A MATTER OF RECORD

Alan Craig, former Scotland Yard detective turned private investigator, is back. This time he is on hand as a mystery junket's expert crime solver. Of the twenty-odd mystery fans who meet in Venice at the start of the junket, nine are from the same English town of Fawchester. They are nine people with nine secrets . . . and one of them is desperate enough to kill in order to keep Alan and the others in the dark.

Books by Malcolm Gray
in the Linford Mystery Library:

LOOK BACK ON MURDER
STAB IN THE BACK

MALCOLM GRAY

A MATTER OF RECORD

Complete and Unabridged

LINFORD
Leicester

First published in the
United States of America in 1987 by
Doubleday & Company, Inc., New York

First Linford Edition
published December 1990

British Library CIP Data

Gray, Malcolm, *1927–*
    A matter of record — Large print ed. —
Linford mystery library
I. Title
823.914[F]

ISBN 0–7089–6998–4

Published by
F. A. Thorpe (Publishing) Ltd.
Anstey, Leicestershire

Set by Words & Graphics Ltd.
Anstey, Leicestershire
Printed and bound in Great Britain by
T. J. Press (Padstow) Ltd., Padstow, Cornwall

About the Author

Malcolm Gray is the pseudonym of a popular and successful British mystery writer. Under his own name, Ian Stuart, he is the author of twelve previous mystery novels, including *A Growing Concern* and *Garb of Truth* published by the Crime Club. A MATTER OF RECORD is his third Malcolm Gray mystery for the Crime Club, following *Stab in the Back.* Mr Stuart is also a bank manager and lives with his wife in Hertfordshire, England.

1

IT was in Venice that Ruth Adamson made up her mind to kill Francesca. She was walking along the Riva degli Schiavoni with Leila Davidson, marvelling at the view and the effect of the sunlight on the water, when the decision came to her quite suddenly. She hadn't been thinking about Francesca, and it seemed to arrive, a sort of *fait accompli,* without any impetus from her, although she supposed that her subconscious mind must have had something to do with it. For a fleeting moment she experienced the unholy joy of a conventional person nurturing an outrageous plan, and she stopped, a strange smile spreading across her pleasant, rather ordinary features. After all, it wasn't often that one resolved to do away with somebody with whom one lived, and who had become a part of one's life. How strange, though, that the idea should come to her now when she was so happy.

A few yards away the boats moored at the water's edge thudded against each other restlessly as they rose and fell in the wash of larger craft. They reminded Ruth of the heads of cattle jostling in a confined space. A *vaporetto* was coming in to the San Zaccaria stop, and beyond it the canal was dotted with an assortment of launches, gondolas, and other water buses with, behind them, the island of San Giorgio Maggiore shrouded in a light heat haze. Ahead, round the great arc of the Riva, were the white dome of the Salute and the entrance to the Grand Canal.

Ruth could hardly believe she was here. After all these years. She and Don had sometimes talked about coming one day, but they never had, and after he died she hadn't wanted to come on her own. Somehow this trip, because it was connected with her work, had seemed different. Even so, she had hesitated

2

when Norma Paget first asked her.

"We're flying out, having four nights in Venice, and coming back on the Orient Express," Norma had explained. "It's going to be a trip specially for people who like mystery stories, and we'll play up the Agatha Christie bit. Other people have done it, and we think it'll be fun."

"It sounds wonderful," Ruth agreed.

"We're asking a man called Alan Craig to go; he's a private detective who used to be in the police. The people in the party will play a sort of murder game, and he'll try to solve it, explaining how the police would work on a real case. Will you come and give a talk?" Norma knew how to be very persuasive. "You know, 'Agatha Christie and *Murder on the Orient Express*'. That sort of thing."

"Me?" Ruth exclaimed, considerably startled. She had taken it for granted that Norma was trying to sell her a ticket for the trip. "Oh no, I couldn't."

"Why not? You're the ideal person, you're a famous author, and you're used to giving talks. Naturally we'd pay a fee and all your expenses."

"No, really."

"Please do." Norma's dark eyes pleaded eloquently. "We're counting on you. You'll be the major attraction."

"After St. Mark's and the Orient Express," Ruth commented drily. "No, honestly."

She had demurred a little longer, but in the end she had capitulated as, she suspected, she had known all along she would. And now she was glad she had come. If she hadn't, she might never have made up her mind about Francesca. It was strange how cool, almost detached a view she could take, she thought. She had just made one of the most important decisions of her life, heaven only knew what the consequences would be, yet she felt quite calm.

Leila Davidson was eyeing her with concern. "What is it, Ruth?" she asked. "Is something wrong?"

Ruth realised that she had stopped and was smiling happily. She must look idiotic. Turning her head as if she were waking from a dream, she said, "I'm going to kill Francesca."

Leila stared at her. "Ruth!" she protested. "You aren't serious?"

"I am."

"You can't. You mustn't."

"Why not? You've no idea how I hate that woman. I loathe and detest her."

"She's not as bad as all that," Leila said. "I rather like her."

"You don't have to live with her day in and day out," Ruth told her bitterly.

The sun was shining from a clear sky, yet it seemed to Leila as if a cloud had suddenly passed in front of it. She glanced at her companion and saw that Ruth had made up her mind. It's crazy, she told herself. She can't mean it.

"I need coffee," she said abruptly.

They had come to one of the *trattorias* along the Riva and she turned into it. Ruth, a little amused by her friend's horrified reaction, followed her. At that time in the morning the open-sided marquee was nearly deserted. They sat

5

down at a table on the sunny side, and Leila ordered two *cappuccinos.*

Looking at her, Ruth wondered how old she was. Thirty-five? Forty? With her slim figure, her shortish blonde hair, and her youthful looks, from across a room Leila could have passed for thirty, but she must be older than that.

"Why did you come on this trip?" she asked when the waiter had brought their coffee.

Leila shrugged. "It looked interesting, and I thought maybe I could do a piece about it for one of the magazines in the States."

Leila was a New Englander, although she had lived in Britain for the last five years. Ruth knew that she would have liked to write mystery novels herself, but, having soon discovered that she lacked whatever small talent it required, she satisfied herself with writing about the authors who did. Women authors; Leila was a staunch feminist. Between times she wrote magazine articles, she did some editorial work and lectured on mystery fiction at two American colleges.

Although the two women lived only a few miles apart, they had met for the first time a fortnight ago when Leila, collecting material for a new book, had spent most of a day interviewing Ruth at her home. Almost her first question had been, "How do you see Francesca's work as a female private eye in the context of her feminist role in society?" and Ruth, who had never considered any of her characters in that way or thought of Francesca as a private eye, was disconcerted and mildly irritated. She wrote about people, not symbols. At least, she hoped she did, and she told Leila so. After that they got on well, and at Gatwick two days ago the American had greeted her like an old friend.

"How well do you know Paula Renton?" Leila asked suddenly now.

"Fairly well," Ruth replied, surprised by the question. "You know how it is in small towns; we're on some of the same committees, and we meet in church on Sundays, but I wouldn't say we're friends exactly. I don't move in her sort of circles. Why?"

"I saw her with Clive Winters yesterday afternoon. They were having drinks at a grotty little place on the other side of St. Mark's."

"What about it?"

"It just wasn't the sort of place I'd have expected to see her. And I wouldn't have thought he was her type either."

"Just because they were having a drink together doesn't mean anything," Ruth protested, half amused and half irritated. It occurred to her that Leila often had that effect on her. "I expect they met by chance, they both wanted a drink, and that was the first place they came to. He must be twenty years younger than her."

"Since when did that make any difference? They looked pretty close to me." Leila laughed. "I'm not criticising her; if that's what she wants, good luck to her."

"If you're suggesting that Paula's having an affair with Clive Winters . . . " Ruth stopped. The idea was so absurd it was laughable.

"Okay, maybe I'm putting two and two together and making a hundred and fifty-eight," Leila conceded, not in the least put out. "It just seemed an odd place for them to go. Almost as if they didn't want to be seen."

"Honestly!" Ruth said. "Paula just isn't the sort for that kind of thing."

Teasingly Leila asked, "Is there a sort?"

"There's a sort who don't," Ruth answered firmly.

"Maybe you're right. But what do you make of our Clive?"

"I don't know that I make anything of him, I've hardly spoken to him. He seems pleasant enough."

"Oh, he's charming, I grant you that. But I get the feeling it's all on the surface. Maybe I'm prejudiced, I knew a man like that once; he could turn the charm on as if he had a built-in switch. It seemed genuine, too."

"Who was he?" Ruth asked, her

annoyance already fading.

"My husband," Leila replied succinctly. She picked up the bill the waiter had left on the table. "Jesus! We save these people's city for them, and they show their gratitude by screwing us for every penny they can. It was only coffee we had, not triple brandies, for Chrissake."

Ruth laughed. Now that she had come to a decision about Francesca she felt a little light-headed. "Venice was founded on piracy," she remarked. "They've been at it for the last thousand years, and they're not likely to change now. You have to accept it as part of the price you pay for all this." She looked out under the awning of the marquee. "It's worth being overcharged a little."

"A little wouldn't be so bad," Leila retorted, taking some notes from her purse and putting them with the bill on her plate. She waved aside Ruth's attempt to contribute her share. "No, it was my idea. It's not the little I resent, it's the lot."

Paula Renton hadn't wanted Betty

Layton's company, and now she wondered how she could escape without actually being rude. She wasn't quite sure why she disliked the younger woman so much. After all, she hardly knew her, and most of the party seemed to like Betty. Was it only that the girl's clear voice, always slightly too loud, offended her, or a feeling that she wasn't as sweet and guileless as she seemed?

Betty was quite pretty, with a round, freckled face and dark brown hair, and she had a friendly, open manner. Her quick, eager way of talking sometimes made her seem a little naive; you could imagine her doing good turns for people on impulse. She and her husband, Harry, had come to live in Fawchester just over a year ago. Harry, the secretary of a largish building company, had chosen to remain at home. He had no interest in mystery novels and disliked travelling.

Paula had been coming from coffee at Florian's when she and Betty nearly collided. She told herself it was ridiculous, she must have imagined that Betty had

11

been watching her, waiting for her to pay her bill and leave before she walked across the square so that they appeared to meet by chance. All because she had twice noticed Betty looking in her direction while she was drinking her coffee and the girl didn't seem to have moved in the last quarter of an hour. She must have done, of course. It was her, she was on edge, ready to imagine almost anything.

"It's a lovely day again, isn't it?" she remarked, smiling politely.

"Oh yes, lovely," Betty agreed. It was only three words, yet she made it sound gushing.

"You're on your own?"

"Yes, most of the others have gone to look at the pictures in the Accademia." Betty grimaced. "I know it's awful, but paintings bore me. Especially really old ones."

Paula, who had been thinking about visiting the Accademia, now made a firm resolution to do so. "Venice is glorious, isn't it?" she said.

"Oh, it's fantastic," Betty agreed rapturously. "I'd no idea it would be so beautiful. You must have been here before, though, hadn't you?"

"Once. But it was many years ago."

Paula's desire to be alone was growing more insistent; she had to think what she was going to do. They had reached the Piazzetta and she turned right, hoping with a fervour which surprised her that Betty was going to St. Mark's or the Doges' Palace. But the girl turned with her.

"Did you know Clive before we came?" she enquired brightly.

Paula had a sudden sense of shock. It was like being hit with something solid, only this went deeper. Forcing herself to speak calmly, she said, "Mr. Winters? No. Why do you ask?"

"I thought you seemed like old friends. He's quite a mystery man, isn't he? I suppose it's because he's so good looking and nobody knows anything about him." Betty giggled. "At least he isn't like our other bachelor. Peter's nice, and I know it's unfair, but you can't help wondering about men of his age when they aren't interested in girls, can you?"

"I thought he was supposed to be interested in the girl who works at the library," Paula commented, trying not to let the hostility she felt show too clearly.

"Is that what they say?" Betty brushed aside the suggestion. "He must be thirty-five at least, and when he's at home he goes everywhere with his mother. Of course, she drinks. Perhaps he feels he has to stay with her in case she does something awful."

"You'll have to excuse me," Paula said, appalled. "I promised my husband I would buy him something while I was here. Goodbye."

Turning, she plunged with almost indecent haste into a side street. For a moment she was afraid that Betty would follow her, but when she looked round at the next corner the girl had disappeared.

Had she been hinting at something,

14

or was it only idle prattle, malicious but comparatively harmless? Paula wondered. She stopped and stared into the window of the dress shop she was passing. That cocktail dress was rather nice, she thought.

One side of the dining room at the Hotel Michele was open to a small courtyard where half a dozen tables were grouped round a rather bare tree. On the other side a glass wall divided it from a private room capable of holding forty or fifty people, and it was there that the Paget Travel party gathered for breakfast and dinner. Including Norma Paget and her husband Michael, a large, fair-haired man who provided the financial expertise for the business and left the promotional side to his wife, there were twenty-two people in the group, and most of them were eating in the hotel that evening.

When Ruth entered the dining room just before 7:45 nearly all the tables were occupied. A number of the people there were still almost strangers to her, for less than half of the party came from Fawchester, and even after two days she hardly recognised their faces. Looking round, she saw with a sense of relief of which she was slightly ashamed that Leila was already seated at a table with the Pagets and Mary Thornton; she wasn't in the mood for Leila's company this evening. Nor, even more emphatically, for Mary's.

Why had Mary come to Venice? She wasn't really interested in crime fiction. Was it for the sake of the journey back on the Orient Express, or to be with Peter Grundy away from his mother's eye?

Five months ago Mary had been appointed deputy head librarian at the Fawchester branch of the county library. She was thirty-two, a thin girl with a mop of frizzy dark hair, a rather long nose, and glasses. At that time Ruth was thinking in a rather vague way that her house was too large for her on her own at her age, and she should do something about finding a lodger. They needn't live in each other's pockets, and the rent would help with the ever-increasing cost of maintaining the old house and ensure that less of it was never used. Old rooms left to themselves soon became musty and neglected.

When one day in the library Mary told her that she had just come to the town from Cambridgeshire and was looking for a flat it had seemed an ideal solution to both their problems. A librarian was unlikely to be a troublesome tenant, Ruth told herself, and Mary didn't look the sort to have wild parties or play pop records loud. She explained that she was thinking of letting two rooms and a kitchen in her house, and a week later Mary moved in.

At first Ruth was rather sorry for her. Living a full, satisfying life herself, the girl's obvious loneliness made her feel slightly guilty. But after a time sympathy and guilt gave way to irritation. It didn't help that, when you considered them dispassionately, the causes were so trivial. The truth was, she thought, living on her own for seven years she had become less tolerant, and now she wasn't cut out to share her house with anyone. It had been her home, hers and Don's, for over twenty years, and now it was no longer quite her own. Moreover Mary wasn't the right person to be her lodger. Staunchly independent herself, the girl's nervousness and clinging manner irritated her intensely. If she was lonely, it was up to her to do something about it, there were plenty of friendly people in the town and organisations she could join. The irritation fed on itself like some obscene creature, growing until at times it became almost an obsession.

Looking the other way, Ruth saw Paula Renton seated alone at a table near the opposite wall. It occurred to her that Paula was often alone. Or did she only seem to be? She was neither unfriendly nor aloof, yet even in a group she had an elusive, solitary air. Perhaps it was her natural reserve. Or perhaps her background made it difficult for people to treat her as one of themselves.

It wasn't snobbishness — they assumed that her problems were different from theirs, and that her interests were, too. Instead of common ground they saw a yawning gap. Some of them probably believed that she spent most of her time at Society parties and West End night clubs.

The Rentons lived at Fawchester Court, a large country house built late in the seventeenth century by a Renton who was a younger brother of an earl. It had belonged to the family ever since. Paula's husband, Colonel Seymour Renton, sat on the boards of half a dozen companies, managed what was left of the estate with the help of a farm manager, and in his spare time played the role in the district he had inherited from his father.

Paula's was the sort of quiet, undemanding company Ruth wanted this evening, and ignoring a waiter who was trying to steer her to a table with Betty Layton, she walked over and asked, "May I join you?"

Paula looked up, saw who it was and smiled. "Of course, Ruth," she said warmly. "Do."

Mrs. Seymour Renton's natural charm had served her well since she was a little girl. She wasn't exactly beautiful, her jaw was a trifle too firm and her mouth too wide for that, but few people noticed it, and at forty-eight she was still a strikingly attractive woman. Her pale gold hair owed only a little to art and her figure was still slim. Ruth, conscious of her own generous hips and rather short legs, envied her that. Also she had never seen Paula not well and appropriately dressed. This evening she was wearing a lovely soft rose-pink dress which suited her perfectly.

Ruth sat down and a waiter came and took her order.

"Have you been over to San Giorgio Maggiore?" she began. Then she stopped.

Paula was looking past her, and after a discreet pause Ruth glanced round. There was only one table behind her. At it were seated four people, an elderly couple and a woman on her own, all of whom Ruth knew only by sight, and Clive Winters. Paula was gazing at Clive, an inscrutable expression on her lovely face.

Ruth remembered what Leila had said that morning. Was it possible that she was right and there was something between Paula and young Winters? No, she couldn't believe it.

Ever since they left Gatwick the other man at the table had seemed determined to attract as much attention to himself as possible, talking too loudly and laughing a good deal too much, a forced, barking sound which set Ruth's nerves on edge. He did it now.

"He's much too much of a good thing," she remarked quietly.

"I'm sorry?" With an obvious effort Paula dragged her attention back to her companion.

"That man at the table behind me."

"Oh. Yes, he is rather, isn't he?"

It struck Ruth that Paula was concerned, even worried. Oh well, it was no business of hers. She started to eat her hors d'oeuvres.

Betty Layton had been one of the first in to dinner and now she was talking to the waiter. *"Fa molto caldo oggi, no?"* she said.

"Si, signora. You would like dessert?" The waiter appeared unimpressed by her Italian.

"Si. Un gelato misto, per favore," Betty told him.

His expression didn't change. "One mixed ice cream," he said.

"Grazie." Nothing, it seemed, could kill Betty's wish to show off her linguistic abilities.

"I didn't know you spoke Italian," the other woman at the table told her. She made it sound like an accusation of some thing discreditable, as if speaking Italian was rather like singing obscene songs in public.

"A little," Betty admitted, with the air of one who is being unduly modest. "I think you should speak the language when you're abroad, don't you? The people like it, although I must say they don't show much sign of it here."

"Perhaps it's your accent," Peter Grundy commented. He was a burly man with dark hair, a florid complexion, and heavy glasses. Almost everything about him seemed awkward, his appearance, his movements, and his manners, and his rudeness now didn't appear to be deliberate. Possibly he realised that he might have sounded offensive, for he added, "They like to show off their English."

Grundy had never wanted to be a teacher, he lacked the necessary patience and he didn't really like children, but his mother had taken it for granted that he would follow in his father's footsteps, and after all the sacrifices she had made in order that he might go to college he had felt obliged to do what she wanted. That, at least, was how he explained it to himself. The truth was that he had lacked the energy or initiative to do anything else. He was not a demonstrative man, and he rarely smiled or showed any emotion, but he contrived somehow to look both discontented and disapproving.

Betty told herself that he was an only child and his mother must have been nearly forty when he was born. That, she thought with satisfaction at her own powers of perception, explained it.

"Have you seen that nice Italian boy today?" she enquired innocently, her clear soprano tones carrying across the room.

Peter looked at her, his heavy features devoid of expression, and didn't answer.

"What boy's that?" the older woman asked curiously.

"I saw Peter with an Italian boy in St. Mark's Square yesterday afternoon," Betty explained. "From the way they were talking, I thought they knew each other. He was such a pretty boy, he'd make a lovely girl with that long dark hair and those gorgeous dark eyes. Don't you think so, Peter?"

"He was trying to get me to buy some postcards," Grundy muttered. There was loathing in his eyes, almost concealed by the thick lenses of his glasses. "I told him I wasn't interested."

"Oh, is that all," Betty said. She laughed brightly.

2

LOOKING out of the window, Craig saw the sea tipping up to meet them. Then the plane came out of its turn and all he could see was the unbroken blue of the sky. Five minutes later they landed at Venice Airport.

It had been sunny but cool in London, with the first hint of autumn in the air. Here it was sunny and warm, and summer seemed reluctant to go.

Craig's invitation had come out of the blue. Norma Paget, telling a friend about her plans for the trip, had mentioned that she was going to ask Ruth Adamson to join the party to give a talk, and she was wondering who else she could enlist to give the project a boost. By chance the friend worked for one of the firms of solicitors who used Alan Craig Associates occasionally and, not very seriously, she said she knew a private detective. Why didn't Norma ask him?

Like Ruth, at first Craig had been reluctant to accept. Up-market jaunts weren't his scene, and ten to one he would make a complete bloody fool of himself. But even if business was brisker than it had been a few months ago, that was a comparative term, and he couldn't afford to turn down any offer of work. So later that day he rang Norma back and told her he would go.

It was his first visit to Venice, and she had booked him on an early flight so that he would have as long there as possible before the party left the next morning. Now, sitting in the stern of the water taxi taking him from the airport to the hotel, he thought that if he were twenty years older he could happily spend a long while here doing nothing very much. But for that he would have to be a lot better off than he looked like being. From what he had heard, he reckoned that all his assets lumped together would last him about a week in Venice. And that was provided he lived frugally. The cost of the taxi alone would have fed him for several days at home.

The boat swerved in a tight arc, shot under a bridge, and stopped abruptly by an iron gate at the side of the Michele. Craig picked up his bag and clambered out.

The proprietor's wife, a handsome lady with a formidable bust, was alone behind the reception desk. "Ah yes, Mr. Craig," she said, looking at a list of names. "You 'ad a good flight?"

"Very, thank you," Craig assured her. He registered, took his key, and walked over to the lift.

As he reached it he was almost felled by a dark, burly man who came charging up the steps from the bar and pushed past him as if he wasn't there. By the time Craig had steadied himself and bitten back the exclamation which sprang to his lips the man had reached the swing doors which led out to the Riva and was pushing through them.

Craig glanced into the bar. As far as he could see, the only person there was a young woman in a print dress and big round glasses. She was sitting at one of the little tables, gazing after the dark man, a look of distress on her thin features. Seeing Craig watching her, she looked away.

The lift came then. Craig carried his bag into it and pressed the button for the third floor.

Emerging from the Accademia, Ruth found Norma Paget beside her.

"It's wonderful, isn't it?" Norma said.

It occurred to Ruth that the other woman's tone lacked enthusiasm. "Wonderful," she agreed. It was, she told herself resolutely. All those magnificent old masters. Only there were too many of them to take in. You should keep coming back, of course, and concentrate on a few at a time. That way, if you knew enough about Art, which she didn't really, you could appreciate them properly. Instead, because you were only in Venice for a few days and there were so many other things to do, you tried to see them all at a single visit. Also, if she was completely honest, religious paintings weren't her favourite form of Art. It was a pity that there were so few Canalettos and Guardis in Venice, you'd think the city would be full of them.

Norma looked slightly guilty. "Don't tell anyone," she begged, "but I've looked at so many Bellinis and Carpaccios, not to mention Titians and Tintorettos, that I have spots in front of my eyes. Half the churches seem to be stacked with them."

Ruth laughed. "I know what you mean," she agreed. "But you must have been to Venice before?"

"Oh yes, several times. But I've always been too busy to see much. I was determined that this time I'd behave like a proper tourist and do all the right things. I've been in St. Mark's and the Doges' Palace, I've visited the glassworks on Murano and I've had coffee at Florian's. I even managed to bully Mike into taking me in a gondola the first evening we were here. And I bought a black leather skirt at a shop on the Rialto Bridge. I ask you, can you see me in a leather skirt with my hips? There's something about this place that makes you throw common sense and reason right overboard." Cautiously Norma eased one foot out of its shoe. "My feet are killing me."

"There's a cafe round there," Ruth told her, nodding in the direction of a corner a few yards away. Her feet hurt, too. Why was walking round galleries and museums always so tiring? she wondered. After all, you didn't really walk very far, and you didn't stand still for long at a time.

"Let's go then," Norma said.

They walked round the corner to the café and she sat down with a sigh of relief on one of the hard, spindly chairs. A waiter who had been talking to a friend in the doorway came over.

"What was all that about at dinner last night?" Norma enquired when he had departed with their order, a cappuccino for her and a *citron pressé* for Ruth.

31

"Last night?" Ruth queried.

"Peter Grundy and Betty."

"Oh, nothing very much. I don't suppose Betty meant it how it sounded." Ruth saw her companion's expression and told herself that, in a sense, Norma was responsible for them all, so perhaps she had a right to know. "Apparently she'd seen Peter talking to an Italian boy the day before," she said. "According to her, he was 'pretty'. She wanted to know if Peter had seen him again."

"The stupid bitch!" Norma breathed.

It wasn't surprising she was angry, Ruth reflected. Obviously she would want the rest of the trip to pass off as smoothly and harmoniously as possible.

"What did Peter say?" Norma asked.

"That the boy was trying to sell him postcards."

"Do you think he's gay?"

"I've no idea. If he is, I can't see that it's anybody else's business."

"Unless it makes trouble while we're out here," Norma commented grimly. She was watching a gondola moving slowly up the canal, its black prow dipping rhythmically like the neck of a swan.

Ruth could see Norma's point of view, but conversations about people's sexual tendencies bored her. Also she found them distasteful. As far as she was concerned, as long as they didn't interfere with other people's well-being, their natures were their own concern. Yet she couldn't quite rid herself of the abhorrence she had been brought up to feel, and she wished that Norma would drop the subject.

"I must say he and Mary Thornton seem very close," Norma remarked. "He only booked at the last minute, when he knew she was coming."

"Do you think they're serious?" Ruth asked. Personally she doubted it, Mary had hardly mentioned Peter to her.

"Heaven knows. But I nearly bumped into them the other evening, and I must say they looked more than just casual acquaintances."

The waiter returned with their drinks,

and for a few seconds neither of them spoke. Ruth told herself that Betty was simply an empty-headed young woman who said whatever occurred to her without considering the consequences. It was absurd to see anything sinister in her tittle-tattle. Yet . . .

"Why do you think Betty does it?" she asked.

Norma shrugged her well-rounded shoulders. "She has to be the centre of attraction the whole time; she's like a little child showing off. Look at the way she insists on trying to speak Italian. She bought one of those cassette courses, and now she thinks she's a fluent linguist. She knows about fifty words, and her accent's terrible." Ruth laughed. "I suppose you've heard her hinting that Mike fancies her?"

"No." It was untrue, Ruth had heard Betty suggesting as much, but she judged it wiser not to say so.

"She's a fool. One of these days she'll say something about somebody, and they'll shut her up once and for all."

Ruth gazed at Norma. There had been something in her tone that shocked her.

Craig was bored. No, he told himself, he wasn't bored, he was tired of his own company. He had spent the afternoon like most other visitors on their first day in Venice, he had been to St. Mark's Square, looked inside the cathedral, strolled through some of the rooms in the Doges' Palace and across the Bridge of Sighs, and taken a water bus to the Rialto where he had walked over the bridge, looking in the shop windows but not buying anything. Okay, he thought, Venice was great. But sightseeing wasn't much fun alone.

By the time he returned to the hotel he was hot and thirsty. He took his time over showering and changing, and when he set out for the bar he felt revived. There wasn't much hope of getting any real beer in the Michele, or anywhere else in Venice, he supposed, but even a lager would go down well just now.

The lift was at the other end of a corridor-like landing with doors on the left and, on the right, three windows looking down into the courtyard restaurant. As Craig passed one of the doors he heard a woman's voice say clearly, "It's this awful uncertainty. Not knowing." It was an English voice, low, well modulated, and not young, and the woman sounded distressed.

Craig walked on reflecting that it was curious how the most innocent remark taken out of context could assume sinister connotations. The woman was probably waiting for some family news, or the result of a medical check, but she might have been the defendant in a murder trial waiting for the jury's verdict.

Michael Paget had suggested that they meet in the bar about seven-fifteen in order that he might introduce Craig to the rest of the party, and when Craig walked in at fourteen minutes past he found nearly a dozen people already there. Paget himself was talking to two

36

women, but, seeing him, he excused himself and came over. "Hallo, there," he said. "Come and meet everybody."

Craig was introduced to people in quick succession. Ruth Adamson he had heard of even before Norma mentioned her, although he had never read any of her books, but the others' names meant nothing to him. Apart from Paget, the only one of them he had seen before was the thin, nervy looking girl in glasses and an unbecoming dress who had been in the bar at lunchtime. He gathered that her name was Mary Something-or-other.

"This is Leila Davidson," Paget told him.

Craig saw a slim, attractive woman regarding him coolly, her eyebrows raised.

"I've never met a private eye before," Leila said.

Craig liked women to be attractive and smart — though when he knew them well somehow it never seemed to matter quite so much — and he grinned. "We're like other people," he told her. "Mostly failures who try."

Leila's eyebrows rose a shade higher and her lips pursed.

"Betty Layton, Alan Craig," Paget said. He was smiling, but perhaps he had sensed something in Leila's manner, for he spoke rather quickly.

"Hallo, Alan." Betty's tone, like her smile, was warm. "You'll have a wonderful time, I know. We're such a friendly group, no snobs or people who won't join in things, you know. Are there, Mike? If you want anything, just ask Mike or me; we'll look after you."

"Thank you," Craig said, wondering who Betty Layton was. Paget, he thought, looked uncomfortable. Glancing round, he saw Norma Paget standing on the top step only a few feet away. She was staring at Betty, and he was startled to see the loathing in her eyes.

Other people were coming into the bar, and Craig was introduced to them: a dark, slightly built young man with alert eyes and a ready smile was followed by a very attractive middle-aged woman with a pleasant, cultured voice. He studied her with interest, certain that hers was the voice he had heard coming from behind a closed door on his way down to the bar. Last came the man who had cannoned into him by the lift when he arrived.

"This is Peter Grundy," Paget said. "Peter, meet Alan Craig, our detective."

"We've already met," Craig told him.

"Oh?" Grundy looked puzzled.

"At lunchtime. I was waiting for the lift and you nearly knocked me over."

"Did I? I don't remember."

Craig hadn't been looking for an apology, and Grundy's bad manners didn't trouble him. He sipped his lager and looked round. The girl Mary was gazing across the bar with a half-hopeful, half-anxious expression. Clearly she hoped that Grundy would join her. But the burly man rather pointedly ignored her and remained by himself, slightly apart from the rest of the party, watching them moodily. Craig remembered what Betty Layton had said and wondered.

Norma had joined a small group including Ruth and Leila. Taking advantage of a momentary lull in the conversation she said, "Shall we go in?" and people began moving towards the dining room.

Craig found himself at a table with Mary Thornton, Leila, and the dark young man, Clive Winters. Winters, he thought, looked a little out of place in the predominantly older, feminine party. He told Craig that he was the sales manager of the Fawchester Brewery Company.

"Is Fawchester your home?" Craig asked him.

"No, I've only been there just over five months. I lived in London before that. It's not a bad little place, though, provided you've got a car." The brewery was owned by a small local company, Winters explained. "We only have ninety pubs of our own, but we supply a lot of clubs and free houses. The Crown's quite a decent bitter."

He turned to Mary on his other side. Watching them, Craig thought that his earlier impression, that the girl was on edge, had been right. She talked too much and too fast, while every few minutes she looked across at the table where Peter Grundy was sitting with three other people.

Winters suggested that they share a bottle of wine. Leila and Craig agreed at once, but Mary asked them to excuse her, she never drank wine.

"I just don't like it, I'm afraid," she explained. "I always drink orange juice with every meal — and just before I go to bed, too." She gave one of her nervous little laughs. "Mike says I'm addicted to it."

"It's better than drugs or tobacco," Winters told her.

"Much better," Leila agreed.

The waiter came and Winters asked him for the wine list.

Leila turned to Craig. "Do you employ any women in your agency, Mr. Craig?" she asked him.

He smiled. "I don't employ anybody."

"Would you employ women if you did?" Leila insisted.

Oh no! Craig thought. Not a damned

women's libber. "Anything to save me doing the typing," he answered flippantly.

Leila's eye acquired a militant gleam. "Is that how you look on women?" she demanded. "As okay to be secretaries and stenographers, but not for anything more taxing?"

"It's what I'd want her for," Craig responded. "I can't type to save my life."

"That's no answer."

"I didn't know I had to answer."

Their eyes met.

"Okay, I'm sorry," Leila apologised.

"I'd employ a woman if she was good at her job and I could afford to pay her," Craig said. "Why?"

"I've met a lot of policemen, and most of them were sexist."

"I'm not a policeman any more. You can't judge them by me."

"What made you quit? Or shouldn't I ask?" Again Leila's tone held a challenge.

Craig wished she would belt up and leave him in peace. Why was she picking on him? There were other men in the party.

"I wanted a change," he said.

It was a prevarication, he thought; true as far as it went, but by no means the whole truth. He had resigned because he was fed up, not with the job, but with what he was required to overlook. And how much choice had he had? When your superintendent doesn't want to know that one of his men is taking backhanders, and puts you down as a troublemaker, you're banging your head against a brick wall if you don't keep quiet. In his case the wall had moved, and he had been pushed out of the way. It would have been different if he'd had real proof, but he hadn't, only evidence. And evidence wasn't enough when the man involved was a CID sergeant with over twenty years service and four commendations.

"Are you glad?"

"Most of the time."

"I guess that's all any of us can hope for." Leila turned to Mary. "Ruth tells me you're writing a book about Fawchester."

43

"I'm going to." The girl's manner brightened noticeably. "It's a really historic place, you know; there was a priory there in the Middle Ages and the Normans had a castle, but it's all gone now. So has most of the priory, there are just some bits of wall left." Mary's diffidence had gone and she spoke with the confidence of the enthusiast.

"You must have to do a lot of research," Clive Winters observed. "I wouldn't mind the writing so much, but all that poring over old papers . . . It would send me round the twist."

Mary laughed. "I love it. That's what takes all the time; I haven't even started the actual writing yet. There are the county archives to examine, and the old parish records, and I've been reading a history a man called Makepiece wrote about eighty years ago. I've been up to St. Catherine's House twice to look up the entries for births, deaths, and marriages, but I'll have to go at least once more. There's so much to check, even with a little place like Fawchester.

But it's all interesting, and I've filled two books with notes already. Mrs. Renton's been very kind. The Rentons have lived at Fawchester Court for centuries, you know, ever since it was built, and she says I can look at the old family records when we get back."

"You haven't done any work while you've been away, have you?" Winters enquired teasingly.

"No, I left my notes and everything behind." Mary smiled sheepishly. "Genealogy's my hobby, and I'm going to bring the Renton family tree up to date. Mrs. Renton's very interested, she says it hasn't been done for a hundred years."

"It looks like you've got plenty to keep you busy," Leila commented.

"Oh, I don't mind." There was a suggestion of boastfulness in the girl's tone. "I love rooting around in old records and looking things up." She seemed to realise that she was monopolising the conversation and stopped, looking slightly awkward, as the waiter returned with their hors-d'oeuvres.

Two tables away Betty Layton said warmly, "I love your books, Ruth. I've read all of them."

"Thank you," Ruth said. You liar, she thought, amused. She would be surprised if Betty had read more than one or two of them, if that. Not without a hint of malice she asked, "Which one did you read last?"

Betty hesitated only a second. "You know, I can never remember titles. Isn't it awful? But there are a lot of people like that, aren't there?"

"Yes, there are."

"And I love them all. They're well, sort of cosy, aren't they?"

Ruth, whose books sometimes dealt with the darker sides of her characters and were by no means cosy, was infuriated. What right had this stupid girl to pretend she had read her books, when all too clearly she hadn't, and use such a patronising term to describe them? But she was too experienced to let her annoyance show.

"You think so?" she asked coolly. "It's the last word I would have used."

Having, in her own opinion, behaved rather well, Betty turned to Paget and said coyly, "You promised you'd take me in a gondola while we were here, Mike, and you haven't. I'm really very disappointed."

"I did?" Paget looked surprised and distinctly uncomfortable.

"You know you did."

"I'm sorry, I — "

"If you're worried about what Norma might think, I understand," Betty told him.

"It isn't that," Paget muttered. "I've been rather busy." Looking for escape, his glance fell on the table where Mary Thornton was sitting.

Ruth, more than a little embarrassed, remembered what Norma had said that afternoon. She might have appeared to dismiss fairly lightly Betty's hinting that Michael was attracted to her, but there had been something almost frightening in her tone when she remarked that if

Betty didn't look out, somebody would shut her up once and for all. Moreover Ruth had seen her expression earlier this evening when Betty told the detective, Alan Craig, that she and 'Mike' would look after him. She had called him 'Mike' again just now. Norma was the only person Ruth had ever heard call him that before, to everybody else he was always Michael.

There were undercurrents here just below the surface, Ruth told herself uneasily. Leila had suggested that something was going on between Paula and Clive Winters. She still couldn't believe that, it was too hard to picture the poised, sensible Paula carrying on even a casual flirtation with anyone, let alone a man like Winters twenty years her junior. No, Leila was letting her imagination run away with her.

Or was she? After all, wasn't it sometimes the respectable, apparently happily married women who suddenly went off the rails? And wasn't it sometimes on account of much younger men, just as middle-aged men did over girls young enough to be their daughters? Ruth, who had never been tempted in that way herself, couldn't believe that Paula would be such a fool.

Then there were Mary and Peter Grundy: perhaps they were more serious about each other than she had thought. Ruth hoped not. Offhand she couldn't think of two people more perversely suited to each other; they were far too alike temperamentally. Yesterday morning Mary had seemed brighter than she had seen her for some time, but in the bar before dinner she had looked absolutely miserable, and it was obvious that Peter was avoiding her. How ridiculous, Ruth thought trenchantly. They were behaving like two love-sick teenagers.

She considered the veal the waiter had just put in front of her. As a rule she wasn't very fond of veal, but Michael Paget's had looked so good she had decided to chance it. Cutting off a small piece, she sampled it cautiously.

3

"**I**'M not sure why trains have such a potent appeal for so many of us," Ruth said. "Certainly they did for Agatha Christie, besides *Murder on the Orient Express* she wrote *The Mystery of the Blue Train* and *4:50 From Paddington*. A train is such a splendid setting for a fictional murder. Especially an express travelling at night between wonderfully exotic cities. It wouldn't be quite the same, perhaps, if it was going from, say, Birmingham to Newcastle."

There was a murmur of amusement; her audience was relaxed and ready to be entertained. Ruth was not a vain person, and she had genuinely expected at least half of the party to slip out rather sheepishly when, at the end of dinner, Paget announced that she was going to give her talk now. But, whether from embarrassment or real interest, they had all remained.

"What more atmospheric setting could a writer of detective stories want than a train like that speeding through the night?" she asked them. "With the thunder of the great locomotives, the clatter of wheels over points, the brightly lit dining cars and, in the *wagon-lits* the heavily shaded lamps casting dark, mysterious shadows. The passengers a group of people shut up together in their little world, unable to escape. Some of them hating others. Very different people, one of them, perhaps a mysterious, slightly sinister foreigner. Because all foreigners in books then were either sinister or ridiculous. Speeding on their way to — what? And all the time, outside the impenetrable darkness."

"Shall we be like that?" Betty enquired brightly. Two or three people laughed.

"Of course," Ruth told her. Damn the girl, she thought. Betty had broken her carefully worked spell. "Ours will be the same train, perhaps even the same coach, in which, just over fifty years ago, that murder was committed. When you go to the dining car, you may walk along the same corridor those murderers walked then," she said. She paused. "Murder is the ultimate crime. It's the taking of what, when you come down to it, is basically all we have, the complete obliteration of one person by another for his or her own benefit. Absolute and final. The traitor may have motives which seem to him adequate, even laudable, but surely nothing can justify planned, cold-blooded murder. Nor excuse it." She stopped.

They were gazing at her, rapt, as if, almost by accident, she had touched a chord which found an echo in them. No, she told herself, that was too far-fetched, a cliché from the sort of novel she despised. Nevertheless for a fleeting moment before she continued she felt the same sense of uneasiness she had experienced earlier, a feeling that there were cross-currents just below the surface which she could perceive only dimly. Cross-currents of emotion, some of them so intense as to be frightening. Perhaps of evil.

She was good, Craig thought. He didn't read detective stories, Dick Francis and Desmond Bagley were more to his taste, but Ruth spoke well, and he was interested in spite of himself.

On his right Leila's only visible reaction was an occasional smile of appreciation. Beyond her Clive Winters leaned across to whisper something to Mary which made her stifle a sudden laugh. Craig had noticed Peter Grundy gaze across at her more than once with a brooding look.

At the same table Paula Renton gave the impression of being somehow a little apart from the people round her. Her face was expressionless, only her eyes moved occasionally. Craig wondered what she was thinking. She intrigued him, she appeared to have herself so completely under control all the time. Was it simply that she was unemotional to the point of coldness? He doubted it, she didn't look like a frigid woman. More likely it was the result of generations of breeding and training; women like her were bred and reared with an aim in view like thoroughbred racehorses. She wouldn't give away anything she didn't want to because she wouldn't let people see what she really felt. He couldn't like women like her, but she fascinated him.

In fact, Craig was wrong.

Ruth finished her talk. Almost without knowing it, she had the born entertainer's talent for leaving her audience wanting more, and she didn't go on for too long.

"She's good, isn't she?" Leila asked Craig.

"Yes," he admitted.

Mary Thornton was going up to speak to Ruth. "That was super," she said enthusiastically.

"Thank you, Mary." Ruth laughed, but she was pleased. At the same time she felt a pang of guilt because the girl was so obviously sincere and she couldn't like her in return. It seemed almost like treachery to dislike somebody who was being so generous. "They listened politely, anyway," she said.

"They were enthralled."

Clive Winters had followed Mary, and he added simply, "Congratulations, Mrs. Adamson. That was great."

"Thank you," Ruth said again.

Other people were coming up to congratulate her, and Mary and Winters moved away to make room for them.

After a few minutes the little crowd began to thin. Craig saw Paula go out of the room, followed almost at once by Grundy. He hesitated in the doorway, and looked across at Mary who was talking animatedly to Clive Winters. She didn't notice him, and after a second or two he turned and walked away through the main dining room towards the lift.

Betty Layton, too, was heading for the door. Mary waited a minute or two longer, then she went to meet Norma Paget who was waiting for her outside the dining room. Winters had already gone.

Craig considered how he should spend the rest of the evening. It was still comparatively early, and he had no intention of wasting the time hanging about the hotel. Venice was geared to visitors, there must be plenty to do here if you knew where to go. Shows, cinemas, bars, sporting events, you name it, they must have it. All the entertainments of a tourist city. He might not know his way around the place, but he could surely find a bar without any trouble, even, perhaps, a cinema showing an American film with subtitles in Italian and the original soundtrack. He headed for the door.

Mary was sitting at a table in the lounge writing a letter. Norma had gone, and she was alone. Craig got into the lift and went up to his room.

When he came down again a few minutes later she was still there, her brow furrowed with concentration and several discarded sheets of the hotel notepaper scattered on the table in front of her. Whatever she was writing seemed to be causing her problems.

Craig pushed through the swing doors and started walking towards the Mole and St. Mark's Square. Lights were burning in the *trattorias* and round the curve of the Riva, and although it was not as crowded as it had been earlier, there were still plenty of people about.

Two girls of about twenty were coming towards him, their skirts swinging. He could hear them talking, chattering in rapid Italian, and as they drew level with him he grinned at them. They giggled and one of them said something to the other that made her laugh. Then they were gone, their heels tapping away over the flagstones. Craig's spirits rose.

At the Ponte Sepolcro he stopped. Old stained walls rose out of the black water and the few scattered lamps cast pools of pale light on its inky surface. Away from the crowds of visitors and its humdrum, day-to-day business Venice was still a mysterious, vaguely menacing city, Craig thought. It was easy to imagine evil here.

"Hi," a voice behind him said cheerfully.

He turned. Leila Davidson was standing

a couple of yards away.

"Hallo, Miss Davidson," he said, deliberately making his tone discouraging. He didn't want Leila's company. The only thing they had in common was their being here in Venice, and it wasn't enough.

"Oh," she said, pretending surprise. Then she grinned. "You thought I was rude at dinner."

"It didn't bother me."

"You were offended."

"Hardly. I've had real experts rude to me too often."

Leila regarded him thoughtfully. "That doesn't surprise me," she said, an edge to her tone.

"Okay," Craig agreed, "you were rude. You meant to be. It's probably part of your technique."

Leila looked startled. "You give as good as you get, don't you?" she said.

"To men usually. Do you want to be treated differently because you're a woman?"

"No. Okay, so I was rude. I'm sorry.

But you bugged me talking like that about women."

"Like what?" Craig demanded. "I just said I'd have a secretary if I could afford one. I would, time I spend typing I could be working and earning money." He paused, half expecting Leila to want to know if he didn't consider typing to be work, but she didn't. "What do you write about?" he asked.

"Authors, mostly."

"Men and women?"

"Women," Leila said tersely.

"You don't call that sexist?"

"Men can write about men if they want to."

"You're begging the question."

"Look!"

"I just asked," Craig said. He turned and stared down into the darkness of the canal. A gondola, little more than a shadow, was coming towards the bridge, the gondolier's arms moving in a slow rhythm. There were two people in the boat, a man and a woman.

"Have you ever been in one of those?"

Leila asked a shade defensively.

"No."

"It's something you should do while you're here, I guess. Like seeing the Statue of Liberty when you're in New York or Buckingham Palace in London. If I don't, I shall feel afterwards that I've missed out on something, and I may never come back. Will you come?"

Craig was startled. "Me?" he asked. "Why?"

"Because you're here, it's our last night, and I'd feel too damned silly on my own."

"You don't like feeling silly?"

"Not too much, if I can avoid it."

Craig grinned. Suddenly he felt more cheerful; perhaps Leila Davidson could laugh at herself after all. "You wouldn't feel half as silly on your own as I would," he told her. "Lying there with a gondolier paddling me along. He might start serenading me!"

"And that would hurt your masculine pride?" Leila wanted to know.

"Too true it would. Anyway, from

60

what I hear, they're a rip off. Do you know how much they charge?"

"So what? You only live once. I'll pay."

"You won't. Equality in everything, right? We share."

"Okay."

They started walking on towards the Mole.

"You know," Leila remarked in the tone of one who has come to a reasoned decision, "you're a very difficult guy."

"I've been told so," Craig admitted.

"And smug with it," Leila said disgustedly.

They had been in a gondola and drunk in Harry's Bar, now, walking back to the Michele, Leila saw a *vaporetto* approaching the San Zaccaria stop.

"There's something great about going everywhere by water," she observed.

They stood and watched the bus edge in to the brightly lit stop. As it came to a halt the gate in the rail was opened and people began to get off. Craig was mildly surprised to see so many passengers; it was well past ten and San Zaccaria was hardly the centre of Venice.

The next moment there was a loud splash, its sound quite clear in the still air. It was followed by excited shouting.

"What do you think all that's about?" Leila asked curiously.

"Somebody mucking about," Craig told her.

"Italians can be excitable."

"More likely visitors who've had a few too many."

Leila was about to observe that Craig was the expert, having been a policeman, but she stopped herself. It would be cheap, and she wasn't in the mood for any more verbal sparring. She felt strangely relaxed, and wondered why. There was nothing special about Craig, for heaven's sake; she had been telling the truth when she said she had asked him to go in a gondola with her because it was their last night here and he was available. There had been no other reason. It was the atmosphere, that was all. This extraordinary place.

They started walking on. When they had gone twenty yards a man passed them, heading diagonally across the Riva towards the Michele's main entrance.

"That was Michael Paget," Leila said. They followed him into the hotel, but by the time they entered the lobby Paget, if that was who it was, had disappeared.

"Would you like another drink?" Craig asked.

"You could persuade me," Leila told him.

Ruth was alone in the lobby reading, and she walked over to her.

"What are you reading?" she enquired.

"*Mansfield Park.* I'd never read it." Ruth smiled. "I don't suppose you approve of Jane Austen."

"Why not? I adore her. Especially *Mansfield Park.* I don't know any woman I've ever felt so much like strangling as Mrs. Norris." Leila glanced round. "Where is everybody?"

"I don't know. Out, I suppose."

"Alan and I have been in a gondola." There was a hint of defiance in Leila's tone. Seeing Ruth's ill concealed surprise, she asked, "Why shouldn't we?"

"No reason," Ruth assured her, mildly embarrassed because she had let her surprise show. After all, she didn't really know Leila all that well, and what she did was her own affair. It was unexpected, that was all.

"He insisted we went dutch," Leila said. "Now we're going to have a last drink in Venice. And if he wants to pay, he can," she added complacently. "Will you come?"

Stifling a ridiculous impulse to say, "You don't want me with you," Ruth slipped a bookmark into her place, closed her book, and stood up, sighing as she did so because these days her back ached if she sat for too long in one position. "Yes, I'd like to," she said.

At that moment Peter Grundy came in through the swing doors and walked across to the lift, pressing the button and

64

getting in when the lift came without taking any notice of the other people in the lounge. He looked even more morose than usual, Ruth thought, and she felt a flash of irritation with Mary.

Betty Layton was at the far end of the bar with a small group of the people Ruth thought of as 'the others,' the members of the Pagets' party who weren't from Fawchester. She was talking in her clear voice, and Ruth heard her say, "Paula, you mean? Oh, I expect she's out with Clive. After all, this is their last night here." She laughed gaily.

The barman came to take Craig's order. As he turned away an apparition appeared at the top of the shallow steps down from the lounge. Ruth heard Craig's muttered exclamation and turned to see what had caused it. For a moment she didn't recognise Mary. The girl was drenched, her clothes were clinging to her, and her hair was hanging lankly round her face. She had lost her glasses, and she was sobbing hysterically.

Craig was the first to act. Striding

across to the weeping girl, he put out a hand and half led, half pulled her into the bar. She came submissively, her shoes making an unpleasant squelching sound.

The proprietor's wife, appearing as if from nowhere, began talking rapidly in Italian. Craig couldn't understand a word she said, but from her gestures he gathered that she was concerned about the water dripping from Mary's clothes on to her carpet.

"Just a minute," he said firmly. "Please."

She gaped at him, but she stopped talking.

"What happened, Miss Thornton?" Craig asked gently. Over his shoulder he called to the barman, "Bring a double brandy, will you?"

The group at the other end of the bar were gazing at Mary in silence.

"Somebody pushed me in the canal." She gulped. "They tried to kill me!"

They stared at her, shocked and incredulous. The barman brought the brandy and Craig held it out to the dripping girl.

"Drink it," he said.

She obeyed, her teeth chattering against the rim of the glass.

"Do you know who pushed you?"

"No. I was getting off the water bus, and I felt a push in my back, hard. There wasn't anything I could do." Pathetically Mary added, "I've lost my glasses."

"Where did it happen?" Craig asked her.

"The stop just along the Riva." Mary shuddered uncontrollably, but she drank the rest of the brandy without being told to. "San Zaccaria, isn't it?"

Leila looked at Craig. "That must have been what — " she began. Then, seeing his warning glance, she stopped.

Craig was thinking the same thing. Allowing, say, ten minutes for the girl to be located in the water and rescued, and the hubbub that would inevitably follow, the timing was just about right. He remembered the lone figure he and Leila had seen walking fast from the direction of the bus stop towards the hotel. Was it Paget? Leila had thought so, but he hadn't seen him so soon, and he wasn't sure. Whether it was or not, Peter Grundy had come in only a minute or two later; he could just as well have come off the *vaporetto.*

I'm going too fast, Craig told himself. And he was taking too much for granted. They didn't know for certain that anybody had pushed Mary. More likely she was simply jostled from behind by other passengers impatient to get off, and she imagined it was done deliberately.

"I do not understand," the proprietor's wife said firmly. "But if everything is all right . . . "

Shrugging, she departed, almost colliding with Paula Renton who had come into the lounge and was standing looking down into the bar. She was wearing a thin summer coat and the light of the big chandelier shone on her pale gold hair.

"Has something happened?" she asked.

"Mary says somebody pushed her into the canal," Betty explained. The brightness of her tone, with its implication that nobody could seriously believe Mary seemed somehow to make the atmosphere more charged.

"Oh no!" Paula breathed, staring at the girl.

Clive Winters appeared at her shoulder. "Been swimmmg, Mary?" he enquired cheerfully. Then, sensing something in the atmosphere, he asked in a different tone, "You didn't fall in the canal, did you? Not really? Because if you did . . ." His voice tailed away.

"She says somebody pushed her," Betty told him.

"They did!" Mary almost shouted it. She had started shaking again.

"The sooner you're in bed the better," Ruth said in the tone, gentle but firm, she might have used to a child. Putting an arm round the girl's shoulders, she led her out of the bar to the lift.

"She'll be all right once she's in bed," Leila observed. "Poor kid, she's had a pretty nasty shock."

It was strange how they all spoke of Mary as if she were a young girl,

Craig thought. She must be over thirty. He supposed that it was a question of personality rather than years, there was something immature and slightly vulnerable about her.

The barman brought the drinks Craig had ordered before Mary's dramatic entrance, murmuring something about it's being a very bad thing to have happened. He refused to take anything for the girl's brandy, and Craig paid him for the other drinks, overruling Leila's half-hearted protest. She seemed subdued.

At the other end of the room the group round Betty were talking quietly, and after a moment Paula walked up to the bar where Clive Winters was sitting alone. Craig heard him ask her if he could buy her a drink, but she shook her head, waited while the barman served him with a Scotch, then asked for a brandy. When the barman had poured it, she paid him and took it over to a table beside the one at which Leila and Craig were sitting.

Craig wondered if somebody had really

tried to drown Mary. The idea seemed preposterous, yet . . . Besides Paget, his wife, Paula Renton, Grundy, and Winters could all have been on the *vaporetto* with her. But what motive could any of them have had?

Behind him Paget's voice said easily, "It's very quiet in here this evening. Where is everybody?"

There was a moment's silence, then Betty said brightly, "Thank goodness you've come, Mike. It's awful, Mary fell into the canal and swears somebody pushed her in on purpose. As if anybody would. It's pathetic, the poor girl so longs for people to take notice of her."

Craig met Leila's eye and saw her lips form the single word "Bitch." He shrugged. Betty's remarks might be objectionable and in very poor taste, but what she said could possibly be true.

Then he noticed Paget's expression; the big man was looking at Betty as if he would like to throw her into the canal personally.

After a moment Paget turned to Craig.

"Do you think we should report this to the police?" he asked. It was clear that he hoped that Craig's answer would be "No."

"I shouldn't think so," Craig said. "We don't know what really happened, and though she had a bad shock, she seems all right now. I doubt if they'd be very interested."

Paget looked relieved. "No, I don't suppose they would," he agreed.

Ruth, standing at the open window of her room, could see away to her left the lights of a big cruise liner moored farther along the Riva. Nearer, almost below her window, people were still strolling over the bridge spanning the narrow canal which passed the hotel's garden. Everywhere there were more lights, on the buoys moored out on the Canale di San Marco, on the island of San Giorgio Maggiore, and a great arc of them curving in a wide crescent round the Riva to the Mole and the entrance of the Grand Canal. They really were like jewels, she thought, sparkling in the soft darkness.

Vaporetti still chugged past every few minutes, and the jostling boats tied up at the water's edge still thudded against each other incessantly. Beyond them Ruth could just make out the slender dark finger of the campanile on San Giorgio and the great dome of the Salute.

Her thoughts returned to the young woman in bed in the next room, and she moved away from the window. Had somebody really pushed Mary into the canal, or had she jumped? It seemed clear that she and Peter Grundy had quarrelled earlier; she was highly strung, had she decided that she couldn't face life any longer, then, when she was rescued, pretended that somebody had pushed her because she dared not admit the truth?

No, she couldn't believe that. Mary might be highly strung, but she had never seen any indications that she was suicidal. If Mary did jump, it was to attract attention to herself. That was possible, Ruth supposed, unlikely though it seemed. But one thing convinced her that it wasn't the truth: Mary was very short sighted. Without her glasses she was almost blind, and although she had a spare pair in her room, Ruth was convinced that she wouldn't have risked losing her usual ones.

Again Ruth found herself wondering why the girl had come to Venice. She wasn't well off, and if it was only to see the city, she could have done that much more cheaply by flying both ways on some package holiday. Was it because she had said she was coming? It was only after she told her about the invitation that Mary had decided to come. No, that was absurd. Yet whatever she had done lately, Mary seemed to be there, dogging her steps.

I'm becoming paranoid about her, Ruth told herself angrily. Just because she lives in my house and I don't like her. It's not even as if she were dangerous or malicious; she isn't, only pathetic and rather sly.

There was too much tension here, she thought. She was letting it affect her. Yet what could be wrong, apart from the harmless flirtations and spiteful gossip which were almost inevitable in a group like theirs? It was all this *Murder on the Orient Express* business, she was letting it colour her view of everything.

Picking up her handbag, she started for the door.

For a while after Ruth's departure with Mary the members of the Pagets' party remained apart, but Paget's entry into the bar drew them together, almost reluctantly, it seemed. At first the atmosphere was strained, all of them there were very conscious how near one of their group had been to death, but gradually it relaxed. Mary was all right now, and nobody took what she had said about being pushed very seriously. Besides, their holiday was nearly over, this was no time to let accidents spoil anything.

It was Leila who started the move

towards unity by asking Paula why she had come on the trip.

Paula smiled a little sheepishly. "I love detective stories," she confessed.

"Do you like Ruth's?"

"Yes, very much."

So, it seemed, did most of the others, and there began a long discussion about the merits of various authors and their creations. Craig saw Leila give him a triumphant grin and smiled back. He knew plenty of men in the Force who were enthusiastic readers, too.

"It's so reassuring to know that the murderer will be caught," a woman said comfortably. "So unlike real life."

Craig happened to be looking at Paula at that moment, and he was surprised to see that she looked anything but reassured. Then she smiled, and he told himself that he had allowed himself to be misled by a momentary change of expression, or a trick of the light. Paula Renton, of all people, must surely believe in law and order.

It was Betty who asked, "Do you

think there's such a thing as a perfect murder, Alan?"

"You mean a murder that's never suspected?" Craig said.

"That's right."

"Yes, it's possible."

"Oh dear." Betty pretended to shiver.

"Suppose you wanted to murder somebody, how would you go about it?" Winters wanted to know.

"I've never thought," Craig replied.

"I'd drown whoever it was," Betty said positively.

The others gazed at her, shocked.

"Betty, you wouldn't!" one of her group exclaimed.

For the first time Betty seemed to realise what she had said. "Oh dear, I shouldn't have told you that, should I?" she said. "Look, here's Ruth, let's ask her. She's invented simply scores of murders."

But Ruth, when asked, answered brusquely, "I've no idea."

"You must have," Betty insisted.

Ruth was angry. She had heard what

Betty said about drowning, and both that and her question seemed to her to be in very bad taste after what had happened. She was determined to do nothing that might be misconstrued as aligning herself with Betty.

The silence became just protracted enough to be awkward. Perhaps even Betty sensed her disapproval. Before it could be embarrassing, Paget asked Ruth how Mary was, and after that the party split into little groups again. But somehow the awkwardness remained.

4

BY breakfast the next morning the atmosphere had changed again. For most of the Pagets' party the journey home on the famous Orient Express was the highlight of the trip, and there was an air of happy expectation in the dining room when Ruth entered it. Even Mary, sipping her inevitable orange juice, seemed to have recovered from her mishap. Norma had gone to her room earlier and persuaded her that she must have been mistaken; Mary herself couldn't think of anyone who might have pushed her deliberately. She couldn't believe that Peter had done it because of their tiff, he was gentle, he would never do a thing like that, and no one else knew her well enough to hate her so much. The thought of Ruth didn't cross her mind.

Ruth told herself that, whatever the

truth of what had had happened. Mary had had a terrifying experience last night. She might easily have drowned trapped under the water bus.

Not everyone was happy this morning, however; clearly there was something amiss between the Pagets. They might assume a professional brightness when they were talking to other people, but Ruth suspected that it was spurious, and they were hardly speaking to each other. Norma looked miserable and as if she had slept badly, and Michael was almost sulky. Ruth liked them both, and she was sorry if things weren't right between them, but there was nothing she could do about it, or about Mary. She was about to embark on a once-in-a-lifetime experience, one that she had dreamed of sometimes, but never thought she would enjoy herself, and she intended to make the most of it.

Having clambered, with varying degrees of composure, out of their water taxis and climbed the broad steps to the Santa Lucia station, the party divided into two groups, each shepherded by one of the Pagets. Some of the women had added vaguely Twenties touches to their dress. Norma was wearing a frivolous little black hat complete with a tiny veil and a red feather, and Betty had on an authentic but unbecoming cloche.

At the Orient Express's own check-in point at one side of the station other passengers were already handing over their luggage and enquiring about their cabins. (Why weren't they called compartments as they were on any other train? Ruth wondered.) There was a good deal of to-ing and fro-ing. She felt herself jostled from behind and turned to find Clive Winters there, smiling an apology.

"Sorry," he said. "Somebody pushed me."

Ruth smiled back, and murmured that it was all right, but she had a sudden horribly vivid picture of Mary being jostled like that as she stepped off the *vaporetto*. Only it would have had to be harder, wouldn't it? So it couldn't have been accidental.

"You feel like coffee?" Leila asked.

Ruth hesitated. "I had two cups at breakfast, I shouldn't really have any more. Too much caffeine doesn't agree with me, and I *can't* make myself like the decaffeinated, but oh yes, let's." She laughed at herself. They headed for the buffet, and she added innocently, "I haven't seen Alan Craig this morning, have you?"

Leila gave her an amused glance. "He's around," she said. "We had breakfast together."

"Oh?" Ruth smiled back. "I thought he handled things very well last night."

"Yes, he did, didn't he?" Leila agreed.

They paid, got their coffee, and carried it over to a table near one of the windows.

"Mary seems okay this morning," she remarked. "Do you believe somebody pushed her?"

"I don't know," Ruth confessed. "She didn't say anything about what had happened after we got upstairs. She hardly spoke at all. Once she was dry and

82

warm the thing that seemed to concern her most was losing her glasses."

"She was lucky," Leila commented. "I read once that the water here's lethal if you swallow it." She paused. "There was a water bus that came in just as Alan and I were passing that stop. We heard a kind of splash and a lot of shouting, but it didn't seem like anything much, so we just walked on. I guess that's when it must have happened. A minute afterwards a man passed us and went into the Michele by the swing doors."

"Did you see who it was?" Ruth asked.

"Sure, it was Michael."

"It can't have been." Ruth stopped. "He wouldn't. He must have been just walking along the Riva like you and Alan."

"I suppose so," Leila agreed. "After you'd taken Mary up Betty started telling everybody that she'd invented it all so that people would take notice of her. Maybe she was right."

"I don't think so," Ruth said slowly.

In the cool light of morning it was harder to envisage any sane person voluntarily jumping into the canal in the dark. Especially just there. And Mary was sane. Moreover she was an intelligent young woman who would have realised the dangers. Quite apart from swallowing polluted water, she could have been crushed between the *vaporettos* hull and the floating structure of the bus stop, or sucked under and drowned. But if somebody had pushed her deliberately, they too must have foreseen the consequences.

It was horrible, Ruth thought. She had known Michael Paget ever since he and Norma took over the business in the High Street more than three years ago. Not very well, it was true, rather as Norma's husband, always slightly in the background. But still it was inconceivable that he should do such a thing.

She sensed some people sitting down at the table behind her, and, looking round, saw Betty Layton and a couple who had been in the bar with her last night.

"We're in Coach 52," the woman said in a discontented voice. "I must say I'm disappointed, I thought all the coaches had names. Why hasn't ours?"

"The *Wagon-Lits* coaches don't," Betty told her. "Only the British Pullmans."

"I'm sure they did on television." The woman still sounded as if she believed that she had been deceived in some way. "Oh well, I suppose it's all right."

"Did you know the Continental train's nearly a quarter of a mile long," Betty told her. "Only they don't call it a train, it's a rake. And there's a staff of forty."

"Really?" the woman said.

It was clear that neither she nor her husband was in the least interested, but that didn't deter Betty, who went on imparting information about the train in her light, clear voice.

Leila caught Ruth's eye and grinned. "Let's go," she said.

At least Betty had been right about one thing, Ruth reflected as she trudged along the platform beside Leila, it was a very long train. And even from the outside it looked opulent in its rich blue livery with its heavy brass lettering.

Their cabin steward was waiting at the bottom of the steps to Coach S1. His name, he told them, was David, and he would come to see them in their cabin shortly.

They climbed the steps to the corridor. In a corner was a small iron stove with, beside it, a bag of charcoal.

"What do you think that's for?" Ruth asked.

"Search me," Leila replied. "Maybe it's to keep us from freezing if we get stuck in a snowdrift like they did before."

Ruth laughed. "That was in Yugoslavia. I doubt if they get snowdrifts like that in Italy in September."

"Oh well, it's as well to be prepared, I guess." Leila was carrying a raincoat and a large shoulder bag. "I'm going to stow these things away, and then I'll get out to take some photographs," she said when they had found her cabin halfway along the corridor. "All right," Ruth agreed.

Her cabin was the last but one in the coach. She put down her handbag and looked round. Until now a journey on the Orient Express had seemed to her rather like staying at the Dorchester or cruising in the Mediterranean on her own yacht, something people like her simply didn't do. Now she was here. Feeling a little like an excited schoolgirl, she examined the cabin's fittings, marvelling at the ingenuity which put so much into so small a space, the array of switches and the intricate marquetry of the panelling. There was a reading lamp on the tiny table under the window with a magazine and a folder containing Orient Express stationery beside it. Time to look at the magazine later, she thought.

Going out to the corridor, she saw Leila on the platform busily taking photographs. Other passengers were boarding the train, and Ruth saw Mary walking with her rather ungainly, loping stride, a drab green bag slung over her shoulder. She was alone, but just behind her was Peter Grundy. It seemed to

Ruth that he was following the girl, but he made no attempt to catch her up before she climbed into the coach. Ruth watched as she came along the corridor, looking for her cabin.

"I must be next to you," Mary said. "Isn't that strange?"

"Yes," Ruth agreed, stepping back into her own compartment so that the younger woman could pass. She was a little ashamed of her own lack of warmth.

"Perhaps Norma did it on purpose," Mary suggested, going into the end cabin. "See you later."

The door closed behind her, and a moment later Leila returned from her photograph taking.

Eventually the last stragglers boarded the train, and at one minute to eleven, just four minutes late, the Venice-Simplon-Orient Express stirred, dragged itself into motion, and pulled out of Santa Lucia station at the beginning of its long journey to Boulogne with its complement of 180 passengers and forty staff.

By the time it passed through Padua forty minutes later the passengers had settled in, their overnight luggage had been delivered to their cabins, and their stewards had come to explain the uses of the numerous switches. Disembarkation forms had been completed, and the head waiter had taken orders for lunch. Some people had already made their way to the bar car in the middle of the train.

Ruth decided that the scenery was unlikely to be particularly interesting for a while and that she would read until lunch. She wasn't used to as much company as she had had during the last few days, and while she enjoyed it, she found it slightly wearing. It was all part of growing older and living alone, she supposed ruefully.

There were two sittings for lunch and dinner, and the Pagets' party were to eat together in the first of them in the *Étoile du Nord* dining car. Ruth read until the train had left Vicenza, then she put down her book and set out for lunch. At the same moment Leila emerged from her cabin, and they walked on together.

"This really is something!" Leila observed admiringly, looking round after a waiter had shown them to a table at one end of the dining car.

It *was* beautiful, Ruth thought, with its brown and white decor, the roof white and the marquetry panels and upholstery dark brown. Glass and silver gleamed on crisp white linen.

Across the aisle and two seats along Betty Layton was regaling her companions with more information about the history of the Orient Express. It was patently clear that they were bored, and Ruth reflected that few people were so tedious as those who insisted on showing off their knowledge of subjects in which one had no interest. Betty couldn't have kept it up ever since Venice, surely?

"Shall we have some wine?" Leila suggested.

"Yes, why not?" Ruth agreed. Not to would be rather like going to a wedding where everybody else was drinking champagne and accepting only water, she thought.

Through the window beside her she could see the clustered orange roofs of villages and oceans of green flat-topped vines, while beyond them, in the distance, were the craggy peaks of the Dolomites. She had always loved eating on trains, and she was beginning to feel wonderfully relaxed, the tensions and anxieties of the last few days draining away from her. Had she, perhaps, exaggerated them in her own mind, making too much of what was really very little?

By the time they finished lunch they were climbing through the foothills of the mountains.

"What are you going to do this afternoon?" Leila enquired as they stood up to go.

"Watch the scenery," Ruth replied promptly. She wanted to discourage Leila from suggesting anything else. "And I shall probably have a nap," she added for good measure.

They started back along the swaying corridor.

"We can't go on like this," Norma Paget said angrily. "People are noticing; I saw the way Ruth looked at us this morning."

Her husband stopped rummaging in his case for the book he had packed to read on the train, and which he knew was there somewhere. "Like what?" he demanded, looking at her over his shoulder.

"Oh, don't be so childish, Mike. You know perfectly well. I stood by you last time, I'm not going to put up with all that again."

Paget straightened up and turned to face Norma. He had gone very white. "What the hell are you suggesting?" he demanded.

There wasn't much room in the cabin for a confrontation, and they were standing with their faces almost touching.

"You and Betty," Norma said bitterly. She mimicked the younger woman's bright tones. "'Mike and I will look after you'. That stupid little bitch! You don't know how ridiculous you look."

Unaccountably, Paget seemed to relax a little. "She's a client," he said. "What do you expect me to do? Tell her to go to hell? I can't help it if she — "

"If she what? Wants to get you into bed with her? Or has she already?"

"I don't even like the little cow," Paget said disgustedly. "You didn't hear what she was saying about Mary last night, suggesting she'd jumped into the canal to make people take notice of her. She's mad."

Norma stared at him. It was the truth, she thought. He really wasn't interested in Betty. But there was somebody. She had known that before they left home, and assumed it was Betty because of the girl's possessive attitude towards him. Now, in a moment of revelation, she saw the truth. There had been clues, she realised that, but at the time they had meant nothing to her. For the last few weeks she had been too busy working in the agency six days a week and planning this trip to pay much attention to anything else. She had assumed too easily that after that other time Mike had learnt his lesson and wouldn't play around with other women again. After all, he did really care for her, she was confident of that. But she should have known him better.

"It's Mary, isn't it?" she demanded. "You persuaded her to come so that you'd he able to sneak off together while you were in Venice, and when you got there you found she wasn't interested in anybody but Peter Grundy." Norma laughed harshly. "My God, that must have hurt your pride, her preferring him to you!"

"For God's sake keep your voice down," Paget said angrily.

"Why? Don't you want anybody else to hear what a fool you've made of yourself?" Norma paused. Then she asked in a different tone, "What do you see in her? That dull, skinny — "

"Shut up!"

"She doesn't even try to make anything of herself."

"Maybe you try too hard," Paget said.

Norma stared at him. "You bastard!" she breathed. "After all I've gone through for you!"

At that moment the engine whistled and the train plunged into a tunnel.

At Brenner the brown Italian locomotives were changed for the orange ones of Austrian Railways and the Orient Express began the long descent towards Innsbruck. Standing in the corridor, Ruth looked out at the peaks and valleys of the Tyrol and thought how beautiful it all was.

A mid-afternoon quiet had settled on the train. Its passengers, relaxing into the routine of a long journey, were mostly in their cabins reading or simply resting. No one else was in the corridor of Coach S1 except a fat uniformed Austrian official who had joined the train at Brenner. Ruth backed into the doorway of her cabin to make room for him to pass. As he did so he said something genially in German and gestured at the scenery. Or was it the road spanning the valley on a viaduct hundreds of feet above the trees? Ruth, who spoke no German, wasn't sure. She nodded and smiled.

A minute or two later Paula came along the corridor.

"Isn't it glorious?" Ruth said.

"What?" Paula looked preoccupied. "I'm sorry?"

"All this," Ruth explained, nodding to indicate the view.

"Oh yes, it's lovely," Paula agreed, but her tone suggested that she had neither the time nor the inclination to admire the scenery.

She went into the toilet at the end of the coach, and the door closed with a slam.

After a few minutes she returned.

"Yes, you're right. It is very beautiful," she said.

They chatted briefly, then she walked on and disappeared into the cabin three beyond Ruth's. Of course, that was hers,

96

Ruth thought. She had seen Paula enter it when she first boarded the train at Venice, and, later, sitting there reading a magazine when she passed it on her way back from lunch and the door was open. The one she had come out of just now was farther along.

Her thoughts were interrupted by the arrival of the steward with tea and pastries, and she returned to her cabin to enjoy them. For a while after that she read.

Near the other end of the coach Craig finished his tea and wondered what he was expected to do tomorrow. All Norma Paget had told him was that the members of the party were going to play some sort of murder game she had devised, and it was his job to try to solve it, finding the clues and questioning the 'witnesses,' at the same time explaining what the police would do in such a case. Privately Craig considered it highly unlikely that they would ever be faced with the sort of crime that he suspected Norma had dreamed up. He was on a hiding to nothing; almost certainly he would fail, and he would look a right burk.

Not that anybody was likely to take the puzzle very seriously, but failure wouldn't do much for his professional reputation. What reputation? he thought. He was kidding himself. All the same, he had better find out as much as he could about the game now, in order to be as prepared as possible.

The Pagets had the next cabin. Craig was about to tap on the door when he heard voices raised angrily behind it, and he stopped. If the Pagets were having a row, he didn't want to know; there would be plenty of time to see Norma later.

As he hesitated Mary Thornton came out of her cabin and entered the toilet next door to it. That was a strange business last night, Craig reflected. If Betty Layton was right, and Mary did jump into the canal, it was a damned silly thing to do. On the whole he was inclined to believe that she had been jostled by somebody behind her who was in a hurry. It would have been natural enough, given the shock and her temperament, for her to imagine that she had been pushed deliberately. Only there was one serious flaw in that theory.

Craig stayed looking out of the window, and when Mary reappeared and stopped to admire the scenery too, he strolled along the corridor to join her.

"It's fantastic, isn't it?" she said.

"Great," Craig agreed.

"Have you ever been to Austria before?"

"No."

"Neither have I."

Whatever the truth of what had happened in Venice, Mary looked to be fully recovered now, Craig thought. Her sort of skin never had much colour, but her eyes were bright, and she sounded as cheerful as she had done at dinner last night. She would never be pretty, but she had good eyes, and if she took a bit of trouble over her appearance, she wouldn't look bad. Maybe she didn't care. Or pretended she didn't.

They chatted for a few minutes, then Craig returned to his cabin and read a magazine until the train pulled in to Innsbruck station. There he joined some of the other people who had got out to stretch their legs and take photographs of the mountains surrounding the city. Twenty-five minutes later the Orient Express resumed its journey.

Time passed slowly and pleasantly for most of the passengers, but Craig, while he could appreciate the luxury, was beginning to find the restrictions of a long train journey irksome. If he had been at home he would have been playing football this afternoon, and this evening he would have had one or two drinks with some of the lads.

So what? He was being well paid for this weekend, and it was better than sitting in the back of a freezing van for hours on some surveillance job. He had done that often enough without griping. It was the people, he told himself. They weren't his sort. Some of them were all right, Ruth Adamson, for example, seemed sensible and down-to-earth, but there wasn't one with whom he had anything in common. And they probably regarded him as an oaf, interesting only because he came from another, rougher world. Crime and criminals always fascinated people who didn't suffer as a result of their activities.

Was Leila Davidson like that? he wondered. Very likely. It was strange that he should have enjoyed yesterday evening with her when he disliked so many of the things she stood for. The truth was she was as sexist and prejudiced as the men she criticised, only she was too bloody blind to see it. To hell with her, she got under his skin.

When the time came to change for dinner Craig donned his evening suit and went along to the bar. It was already crowded with men and women in evening dress, and the pianist playing a selection of Cole Porter tunes was almost drowned by the buzz of conversation. Craig worked his way up to the bar and bought himself a Scotch. As he turned away with it he almost collided with Clive Winters doing the same.

"It was never like this on the old five twenty-five," Winters remarked with a grin.

"Five twenty-five?" Craig queried.

"From St. Pancras. I worked in London before I got the job at Fawchester, and I used to go home at weekends." They found two vacant seats and sat down. "You didn't get many dinner jackets on the 5:25 either."

"I shouldn't think so," Craig said, sipping his whisky. He didn't particularly care for the younger man, Winters was too much the smooth salesman for his taste, but at least he was more at home with his type than with the others, and he was quite glad of his company.

"You're doing your party piece tomorrow, aren't you?" Winters asked him.

"Yes."

"The best of British. Do you know what our Norma's cooked up for you?"

"Not really."

"Murder's not my game, I'm afraid. Too gruesome."

Paula Renton came into the car, elegant in a lacy black dress, and the two men stood up as she stopped by them.

"Let me get you a drink, Paula," Winters said. "And take my seat. What will you have?"

Craig saw Paula frown.

"Nothing, thank you," she said. With a fleeting smile at Craig she walked on.

There had been no mistaking her annoyance, and Craig wondered what had caused it.

"I must have a word with Michael Paget before dinner," Winters said, draining his glass. The snub didn't seem to have bothered him. "See you later."

He walked away, and Craig sat down again. A fat woman in a black jacket striped with shiny silver took the seat Winters had vacated and started talking loudly to the man with her. Craig finished his drink and decided that the crush round the bar was too dense to make it worth the effort to get another. Some of the Pagets' group were already making their way to the dining car, and he joined them.

Several of the women were wearing short Twenties-style dresses with long ropes of fake pearls. Craig saw Betty Layton in green lavishly decorated with gold sequins. There was a green velvet band round her freckled forehead and long green pendants hung from her ears. With her green eye-shadow she looked rather like a snake sloughing its skin, he thought.

She saw him at the same moment. "Alan!" she cried. "Come — "

Craig, who had no intention of joining her and her two companions if he could help it, smiled briefly and walked on before she had time to finish what she had been going to say.

Leila, resplendent in an ivory coloured dress, was sitting alone at a table for four a little farther on. "Hi!" she said. "Are you going to join me?"

Craig sat down opposite her "You can

put up with a chauvinist ex-copper?" he asked.

"I can try," Leila told him. "Ruth will be coming soon, I guess."

In fact she arrived almost at once, looking slightly flustered and unsure of herself. She had long been convinced that the only things which suited her, and in which she felt comfortable, were jerseys and skirts, and that for her to dress up for dinner was a waste of time and effort. This evening, however, she had felt that she owed it to the Pagets to make a gesture, and she was wearing a dark red dress with a low waistline and a pleated skirt which she was sure was far too young for her, but which in the shop had seemed vaguely Twenties-ish. She had put on a string of white imitation coral and taken more trouble than usual with her hair so that it softened her rather square features.

"Ruth, you look stunning!" Leila told her.

"Nonsense," Ruth replied stoutly. All the same, she felt herself blushing with pleasure. She had been a little afraid that she might have to share a table with people she didn't like, and it was a great relief to find herself with Leila and Alan Craig. He seemed rather nice, she thought, intelligent and a lot more thoughtful than he probably liked people to think.

The coach was soon alive with the buzz of talk and the chink of cutlery. Many of those in the *Étoile du Nord* car were members of the Paget Travel group; they had come to know each other fairly well during the last few days, and there was almost a party atmosphere.

Ruth and her companions were nearly halfway through their hors-d'oeuvres when she saw Clive Winters come in, followed almost at once by Paget, the last of their party.

Shortly afterwards the Orient Express passed through the station at St. Anton and entered the Arlburg Tunnel. By the time it emerged again dusk was closing in. Ruth could see the sky in the west tinged with a rosy gold, while on the other side of the valley the mountainside was lost in shadow and far below lights shone like stars in the dusk. Soon, she thought, it would be quite dark.

107

5

IT was illogical to feel this sense of foreboding, Ruth told herself. All around her in the bar people were enjoying themselves. It wasn't a noisy crowd, but the air of quiet gaiety there had been at dinner still prevailed. Most of the people here would never travel on the Orient Express again, and they intended to make the most of the experience. Alan Craig was with two other members of the Pagets' party, a youngish couple from Bedfordshire, and they certainly seemed to be having a good time.

"Do you ever get a feeling that somebody's following you round?" she asked Leila.

Leila laughed. "No. If I did, I'd start worrying there was something wrong with me." Sensing something in Ruth's manner, she studied her more closely. "What is all this, for heaven's sake?

Are you working on ideas for a new book?"

"No." Ruth forced a smile. "Would you say I was paranoid?"

"You? Jesus no. Why? Do you think somebody's following you around?"

"Not really, I suppose. It's just that everywhere I go, Mary seems to be there too. I expect I'm just imagining it. I'm not used to having anybody else living in the house, and I keep running into her. She doesn't go out much."

"It was her you really meant that day in Venice, wasn't it?" Leila asked. "When you told me I didn't have to live with her day in and day out? You were talking about Francesca, but you were thinking of Mary. You don't like her much, do you?"

"No," Ruth admitted.

"It could be that's what it is. If you liked her you wouldn't feel she kept intruding like you do now. What is it about her? I must say she seems pretty harmless to me."

"She's always asking questions about

109

people. Prying. I said, I probably imagine most of it, but sometimes I feel like strangling her."

Leila laughed. "I reckon we all feel like that about other people sometimes," she said. She looked across the bar to where Mary was sitting next to Clive Winters. "I must say she looks okay now."

"Yes," Ruth agreed. Mary looked unusually vivacious, she thought. Perhaps it was whatever she was drinking; no orange juice for her this evening.

She looked past Mary and saw Peter Grundy by himself a few feet away. His expression shocked her. It was a long time since she had seen such naked hurt and resentment on any man's face. As if he felt her looking at him, he stood up and walked out of the coach.

The train roared on, swaying over points. In here all was light and cheer, but out there was darkness and the night, Ruth told herself. They were like the characters in some old film, carelessly making merry while they were borne on into the unknown.

The pianist started playing *"Smoke Gets in Your Eyes."*

Ruth slept badly that night. She had expected nothing else, she rarely had a good night's sleep on her first night in strange surroundings. It was as though her subconscious mind allied itself with her nerves and muscles to revenge itself on her for leaving home. But tonight she minded less than usual; her bed was comfortable, and it was rather exciting lying listening to the sounds of the train racing through the darkness, the roar of the engines, the clatter of the wheels on the track, and the creaking of the coaches. Then there were the occasional stops in the middle of the night at unknown stations with their lights and men shouting in a foreign language.

Somebody passed her door. Another wakeful passenger on their way to the toilet, Ruth supposed. Or perhaps it was the steward, David, summoned to a cabin farther along the corridor. She switched on the light over her head and looked at her travelling clock. It was five minutes past three.

She had made her decision, she told herself. For better or worse. But she couldn't remain in the comfortable security of her bunk for ever, soon she must emerge and face up to the consequences of what she had done. It was all symbolic, of course, and perhaps the danger was less than she imagined, lying here in the dark. Imagined fears. Like the imaginary menace she had conjured up in her talk. But were they all imagined? What had really happened to Mary in Venice? Could somebody have tried to murder her? If so, the would-be killer could be one of their party, here on the train now.

The footsteps returned, stealthy sounding. Ruth was too wide awake to sleep, and she no longer wanted to lie here thinking. Picking up her copy of *Mansfield Park,* she began to read. After ten pages she put down the book and switched off her light, and within a few minutes she was asleep.

Craig was shaving when the tap came on his door. Assuming that it was the steward, he called, "Come in."

But it wasn't the steward who came, it was Paget, pale under his tan and with a haunted expression.

"Morning," Craig said cheerfully. He felt his chin and, satisfied, unplugged his electric shaver. "What can I do for you?"

For a moment it seemed that Paget couldn't find the words to explain why he was there, then he blurted out, "Something's happened."

Craig turned away from the wash basin. "Oh?" he said.

"It's terrible. Mary's dead; it looks as if she killed herself. Can you come?" Paget sounded distraught.

During his time in the police Craig had become accustomed to seeing sudden and violent death in many forms, nevertheless he was shocked.

"What do you want me to do?" he asked.

"You're more used to dealing with this sort of thing than the rest of us," Paget said.

"This is France, I don't know anything about the procedures here," Craig protested. "Who's in charge of the train?"

"M. Bertrand. He's the train manager."

"Then he's the man you want."

"He's there now, but I'd be grateful if you'd come too."

It occurred to Craig that Paget looked more stricken than he would have expected him to be. And there was something there besides shock. What was it?

"All right," he agreed reluctantly. Paget probably wanted moral support as much as practical help, he thought. Perhaps more. "Give me a minute."

Paget waited while he washed and put on a shirt. "How did she do it? If she did?" Craig asked.

"An overdose, it looks like. There's

an empty pill bottle in her waste-paper bin."

"So it could just as easily have been an accident."

"I hope to God it was," Paget said fervently.

Usually in these circumstances, Craig reflected, people insisted from the outset that the death was an accident, even in the teeth of the evidence, rather than face up to the possibility of suicide. Paget seemed to have taken it for granted that Mary had killed herself. Why? True, as far as he knew, they weren't related, but surely as one of the organisers of the party he might have been expected to take the usual line?

"Right," he said.

Outside in the corridor there was a strong odour of burning charcoal.

"What's that smell?" he enquired.

"The steward's stove," Paget answered. "They use them for heating water."

The big man leading, they walked past the closed doors of the other cabins. Many of their occupants were probably

115

still in bed, Craig thought, unaware of what had happened only a few feet away.

"There's a doctor in our party," Paget told him. "Philip Davies. He's in there now."

A thick-set, dark-haired man was standing outside the door of the end cabin. Craig remembered him as someone he had noticed once or twice since he boarded the train without knowing who he was.

"This is M. Bertrand," Paget said.

"Good morning, monsieur." The Frenchman nodded gravely and opened the door for Craig to enter the cabin. Paget, whether from choice or because there was little room for him, remained in the doorway.

Mary was lying on her back, her head turned to the left and her right arm outside the bedclothes. A tall, thin man with greying hair who had been stooping over her straightened up when Craig came in and eyed him disapprovingly.

"This is Alan Craig, Doctor," Paget told him.

116

The doctor nodded without speaking. His expression showed clearly that he had grave reservations about Craig's being there, and Craig guessed that Davies wondered why Paget had asked him to come. Which made two of them, he thought.

He looked round the tiny compartment, which was virtually identical to his own. On the table under the window there was a large plastic container half full of orange juice, a paperback edition of *Ulysses* and the standard folder of Orient Express stationery provided in all the cabins. The wastepaper bin was empty save for some soiled tissues and a small clear plastic bottle which looked as if it had once contained pills. As Paget had said, it was empty now, and the cap was on it. That meant nothing, Craig knew; there might have been only one or two tablets left in it. On the other hand, some suicides were meticulously tidy. He didn't want to touch the bottle, and as the label was on the under side he couldn't see what the pills had been. Not

117

that it probably made any difference.

A drinking glass in its holder by the wash basin still held drops of water, as if Mary had rinsed it out after drinking her orange juice before she went to bed. Possibly she had taken the pills with the juice, or crushed up in it.

There was a small pile of clothes, neatly folded, on the stool, and the fawn jacket she had worn yesterday was hanging from a peg behind the door. Craig felt in the pockets.

"Are you looking for anything in particular?" the doctor asked disapprovingly.

"Yes," Craig answered. "This." He held out a small sheet of paper folded into four. The other men watched as he unfolded it.

It was a sheet of Hotel Michele notepaper. The note itself was brief, written in a girlish, rather spiky hand. "'It's all too much for me to bear'," Craig read aloud. "'After what you did today I know there's no future for us, and I don't want to go on. This is the only way I can find peace. Goodbye'."

After he stopped there was silence. Paget had gone even paler.

"I'll take this for a minute or two," Craig said.

"Should you?" Paget looked uneasy. "I mean, won't the police mind?"

"They won't know, unless you tell them."

"Why do you want it?"

"To check the writing. I'll put it back as soon as I have."

"But why . . . ?" Paget began. "I mean, it's obvious she killed herself. Why do you want to check her writing?"

"To make sure it is hers." Craig stopped. He hadn't been drunk last night, not by a long way, but it had been a good evening and he had drunk a fair amount. Moreover he had mixed his drinks, with the result that this morning he had a headache. When he woke up it wasn't much, but now it was getting worse, and Paget's objections weren't helping. "Look," he said roughly, "you asked me to help, and I'm doing my best

119

to. If you don't like the way I'm doing it, okay, I'll leave everything to you. I didn't want to get involved."

The doctor frowned but said nothing. Paget gave him a helpless look, found no support there, and turned back to Craig.

"I'm sorry," he muttered. "You know best."

"Right."

Craig went past him out to the corridor where the train manager was still standing, effectively blocking off that end of the coach. "What are you going to do about this?" he asked him.

"The train will stop at the next town, m'sieur," Bertrand replied. "The police and a doctor will be waiting there, and they will take Mademoiselle to the mortuary. M. Paget says that 'e will go too, to 'elp the police and attend to the formalities."

Craig nodded. Obviously Bertrand wanted as few of the other passengers as possible to know what had happened. That was both understandable and sensible.

"That's Mrs. Adamson's cabin, isn't it?" he asked, indicating the door next to the dead girl's.

"Yes, m'sieur."

Craig knocked on it. After a brief pause it was opened a few inches and Ruth appeared in the gap clad in a pink dressing gown, her hair a little dishevelled.

"Oh, it's you," she said. "I thought it must be the steward."

"I'm afraid I've some bad news," Craig told her.

"Oh no! I thought there'd been a lot of coming and going." Ruth noticed the train manager's back only a few feet away and Craig saw the apprehension come into her eyes. "What's happened?" she asked.

"Miss Thornton's dead," Craig said quietly.

"*Mary!* Oh no! You do mean Mary?"

"Yes."

"How?"

"It looks as if she took an overdose of sleeping pills."

"On purpose, you mean?"

The train jolted over some points and Ruth put out a hand to support herself. For a moment Craig was afraid that she was going to faint, then he realised that she was only steadying herself because of the train's swaying.

"It seems like it," he said.

"But she was so happy last night," Ruth protested sadly. "At least, I thought she was."

"She left this." Holding the letter by its edges, Craig held it out so that Ruth could read it. "Do you know if that's her writing?"

Ruth scanned the brief note without really seeing what she read. It was as if her mind had erected a barrier to stop her taking in any more. But she recognised the writing. "Yes, it's hers," she said quietly.

"Thank you." Craig refolded the paper, reflecting that Ruth hadn't asked him if he knew the identity of the 'you' in it. Perhaps she guessed.

"I never dreamed," she said. "Apart

from everything else, the shock and that, it makes you feel so dreadfully helpless."

"Yes," Craig agreed.

"I'll get dressed. Perhaps there'll be something I can do."

Craig told himself that the impression he had formed on Friday night when Ruth swept Mary off to bed, that she was a sensible, competent woman well able to deal with crises, was confirmed. It was only natural that she should be shocked and distressed, but she had stayed calm.

Paget and the doctor were still in Mary's cabin.

"It's her writing," Craig told them. He returned the note to the pocket where he had found it. "It's as well to be sure."

They stared at him.

"My God!" Paget muttered.

"Are you going to tell the rest of the party?" Craig asked him.

The big man pulled himself together. "Norma's doing it now," he answered. "She's just saying that Mary was taken ill during the night and died. We thought that was best."

Craig nodded. "I don't think there's anything else I can do now," he said. "And the French police won't want to find me here when they come. I'll be in my cabin if you need me."

"Right." Rather awkwardly Paget added, "Thanks for your help, anyway."

The row of identical brown doors were still closed, giving the corridor a shuttered, deserted look, and the air was heavy with the scent of burning charcoal. Craig started back towards his cabin.

Before he reached it the train slowed, passed some extensive sidings, and ground to a halt alongside a platform. He looked out. By now it was broad daylight, but so early on a Sunday morning the station was almost deserted, and he could see no sign to tell him where they were. All along the train heads appeared out of windows as people tried to see why they had stopped.

Craig watched a uniformed policeman climb up into the coach and disappear into the end compartment. A moment later an elderly man in plain clothes and carrying a black bag followed him. Two more men in uniform waited on the platform beside a wheeled stretcher.

As he turned to enter his own cabin, Craig saw Norma coming through from the next coach. Without any make-up, her hair less immaculate than usual, she had an oddly peeled, vulnerable look. He guessed that, besides her sense of shock, she was concerned about the effect Mary's suicide might have on her business.

"I'm telling our people," she explained.

Craig nodded. "Mike told me."

"It's awful, isn't it? Poor Mary."

It struck Craig that, while she was shocked and anxious, Norma's grief didn't go very deep. She tapped on the door of the end cabin, which was occupied by an elderly couple named Simpson from North London, and he heard a voice answer as he went into his own compartment.

A few minutes later the stretcher was

brought up to the door at the other end of the coach and Mary Thornton was wheeled away. Michael Paget, looking somehow smaller, went with her carrying a small suitcase, and almost immediately the Orient Express resumed its journey.

Perhaps Norma had been less reticent than her husband believed, however it happened it was soon general knowledge amongst the Pagets' party that Mary had died of an overdose. No one, not even Betty Layton, was insensitive enough to enquire whether they would still play the murder game, and a fairly subdued group took its place for brunch in the *Étoile do Nord* coach. Like Ruth, sharing a table with Paula Renton, Leila, and Craig, they were uncomfortably aware of the two empty seats.

Peter Grundy, alone at a table for two just across the gangway, looked miserable and resentful in about equal proportions, Craig thought. He was toying with the smoked salmon and scrambled eggs the waiter had just put in front of him.

Suddenly, pushing his plate aside, he said loudly, "I can't eat this stuff," and getting to his feet, he blundered off along the aisle, nearly colliding with a waiter coming the other way.

At the table she was sharing with three other people, Betty Layton saw his agonised expression as he passed. "Poor Peter," she remarked in an audible undertone. "He must feel dreadful."

"Why?" the other woman asked. She and her husband weren't from Fawchester, and she knew nothing of Grundy's relationship with the dead girl.

"Well, after the row he and Mary had on Friday," Betty explained. "I mean, why else should she do it? That's why she jumped into the canal, to make him sorry."

"Jumped in, you say?" the woman's husband asked.

"Well, she must have done. Can you really see anybody pushing her? I mean, why should they?"

"I thought she seemed much brighter

yesterday when I saw her," the second man at the table observed. He didn't like Betty, and he was sharing a table with her now only because he was friendly with the other couple and had been talking to them when Betty more or less shanghaied them to join her.

"She did," Betty agreed. "But they say that's the most dangerous time, when they seem to be getting over their depression."

Ruth could hardly help overhearing her, and she wondered why she should find what Betty said in such appalling taste. After all, most of it was the sort of thing people did say in these circumstances. Perhaps, she thought, it was the way Betty succeeded in investing her comments with a ghastly sort of relish. It must be unconscious, surely?

She recalled her first thought when Craig told her what had happened, that the wrong person had died. Perhaps subconsciously she was remembering what Norma had said about somebody shutting up Betty once and for all if she didn't look out. But that was absurd, people weren't murdered merely because they were troublemakers. And, anyway, Mary hadn't been murdered, she had killed herself. There wasn't any connection.

"You could see she was highly strung," Leila remarked quietly. "I guess she was more disturbed than we realised."

"Yes," Paula agreed.

Paula wasn't her usual self this morning, Ruth thought. There was an edginess about her. Yet at the same time, however hard she tried to conceal it, she seemed relieved about something.

I'm becoming far too given to ridiculous fancies, Ruth admonished herself. It must be a sign of incipient old age.

The waiter brought their next course and she eyed the broiled lobster on her plate doubtfully. She liked lobster, although she rarely had an opportunity to eat it nowadays, it was so expensive, but this morning the sight of the succulent pink shellfish belly side up on her plate revolted her. Other people, she saw, were eating it quite happily. Some of them were even drinking champagne, as if they had something to celebrate. She couldn't blame them, they had known Mary very slightly, if at all, nevertheless . . . Ruth took a little lobster on her fork and swallowed it with difficulty.

"It's hard to accept, isn't it?" Craig said.

She turned her head, surprised by his tone, and saw that he was watching her. After all, she thought, he had been in the police, he must be used to this sort of situation. They said that policemen acquired tough skins to protect themselves, they had to, or they would crack up, but Craig had seemed to understand.

"The death of someone close to you," he explained.

"I don't think we were very close," Ruth told him, determined to be honest about it. "She'd lived in part of my house for several months, and I suppose that I should have known her well, but I didn't. Not really. I don't know much about her at all. I'm not a very good neighbour, I'm afraid; I rather value my privacy. It's her killing herself that's hard to accept. Realising what a terrible state she must have been in, and that perhaps I could have helped if I'd seen."

"You couldn't have done anything, honey," Leila said. "Nobody could have told yesterday what she was going to do."

"There's no question that she did kill herself?" Paula asked. They looked at her curiously, and she went on, more nearly flustered than Ruth had ever seen her, "I mean, it couldn't have been an accident?"

"No," Craig told her. "She left a note saying she couldn't go on."

"Oh."

"Did you know her, Paula?" Leila asked.

"Only very slightly. I'd spoken to her once or twice before we came away, that's all."

"She said you'd been very kind."

"I had?" Paula looked startled. "How?"

"Offering to help with material for her book."

"I didn't do anything. She came to see me about it, and I suggested that she might like to look at some of the old papers we have. She seemed quite a pleasant girl, I thought."

"A pleasant girl," Ruth repeated to herself. It savoured of damning with faint praise, and pleasant wasn't the word she would have used to describe Mary. What would she have said?

"Did you know that Mary took sleeping pills?" Craig asked her.

Ruth dragged her thoughts back. "No, but I'm not surprised," she answered. Half reluctantly she took another small piece of lobster as the train sped on, faster now that they were clear of the Paris suburbs, towards Boulogne.

6

CRAIG didn't mind Monday mornings. When he was in the Force, working all sorts of hours, what a day was called hadn't made much difference, time off had been something to cherish and make the most of whenever it came, and now that he worked a five day week and there weren't always enough jobs to fill the time weekends dragged. Usually he had one or two drinks with friends on Friday evenings and played cricket or football on Saturday afternoons, sometimes Sundays too, lingering on in the bar afterwards because there was nothing to go home for. No one to go to. Most of the other lads had wives or girl friends who came to join them before they went out together in the evening, and Craig felt conspicuous alone. He had heard one of them once telling a new girl friend, "His wife was killed in a car crash last year." They understood and, although he didn't want their sympathy, he was glad of that because it saved him explaining or, worse, the suspicion that he was in some way odd.

There had been girls during the last fifteen months, but none of them was serious enough to start him thinking about marrying again, or to prevent him comparing them unfavourably with Jean. In his darker moments he saw himself drifting through life like a rudderless ship; he was thirty-five, and it was time he got himself sorted out.

He told himself so again this morning as he ran down the steps of the multi-storey car park, turned left and walked along Holborn to his office in a side street.

Georgie was in the cubbyhole where she functioned as telephonist and receptionist for the firm of electrical contractors from whom Craig rented his two rooms across the landing.

He stared at her in wonder. "Strewth!" he breathed.

Georgie was twenty and pretty in a pert, chirpy way. The last time Craig had seen her, just after 5:30 on Friday, her hair had been its natural dark brown. Now one side was a vivid magenta and the other half black and half a straw-like blonde. Black and magenta ends, plastered to her forehead, made a saw-toothed fringe from under which she peered out through thickly mascaraed lashes. She had changed the colour of her hair before, but never as dramatically as this.

"What's the matter then?" she demanded defensively.

Craig grinned. "When's the fancy dress party?"

"You don't 'ave ter be rude." Georgie tossed her head, setting the four inch long column of imitation jade which hung from her left ear swinging alarmingly. It looked to be in grave danger of flying off, taking her ear with it. Her other lobe boasted three small gold rings, accentuating the lopsided appearance created by her hair. "My boy-friend likes it any 'ow," she said.

"Ray?" Craig thought that Ray, a normal seeming young man who worked in the men's outfitters round the corner, had never shown such bizarre tastes before.

Georgie looked puzzled, as if the name were new to her. Then her face cleared. "Oh, 'im!" she said scornfully. "'E was months ago. There's bin Terry since 'im."

"Oh yes, Terry," Craig agreed. Hell! he thought. He was still young, wasn't he? Georgie made him feel like an old man.

"I 'aven't bin out with 'im for nearly a fortnight. It's Con now. 'E's different."

Craig could see that. "Let's hope he never is," he remarked cheerfully.

"Is what?" Georgie demanded.

"A con."

"Coo, sharp this morning, aren't we? If yer don't watch out, you'll cut yerself." Ceorgie feigned disgust.

136

"If yer want ter know, 'e's Irish. 'Is name's Con O'Rourke."

"I don't believe it," Craig said. "No real Irishman has a name like that. He's having you on, Georgie."

"You're jealous, that's your trouble."

"I didn't think you knew." Craig grinned. "Are there any messages for me?"

"D'you expect any?"

"While there's life there's hope."

Georgie regarded Craig sympathetically. She had a warm heart, and she liked him. She sometimes thought that if he'd been about ten years younger she could have fancied him something rotten. He was all right, and he wasn't too bad looking either. Not handsome, but kind of rugged.

"Les told me not to let you forget Friday's rent day," she said.

"When did I ever forget?" Craig asked with an air of injured innocence.

"It's not just remembering, it's paying," Georgie told him. "Are you goin' ter be in for coffee this morning?"

"Yes, please." Les owed him a coffee for his crack about the rent, Craig thought.

He crossed the landing to a door bearing a white plastic plaque inscribed in large black letters 'ALAN CRAIG ASSOCIATES' and let himself in. There were no Associates and the outer office had a bare, rarely used look matched by the desk which Craig had bought cheaply from a secondhand dealer in New Cross. It needed a secretary behind it, he thought. A smart blonde, her slim legs showing to advantage when she came in to take dictation, would do wonders for the firm's image, to say nothing of his morale. Clients would see that he was successful.

For the moment he wasn't. Nevertheless things were looking up, and work was coming in a lot more regularly than it had done a year ago. Three or four solicitors used him, as well as several tradesmen and branches of three of the four big banks. Usually it was to trace debtors who had disappeared, or simply ignored letters and threats to take them to court. Once in a while he was asked to find a missing person, or to do something for another firm in the provinces which had no London office. So far he had never been asked to investigate anybody's background or private life, and he was glad, it smacked too much of prying.

Looking up or not, he reflected wrily, all he had in hand at the moment was a report to a bank on a customer who had left them with an overdraft of £467, was living in a lodging house in Kentish Town, and claimed that he was out of work. Craig, who had seen his room, believed him. If he took his time, allowing for typing out his account as well, he could make the report last half an hour, but it would take some doing.

He switched on his answering machine. An enquiry agent in Manchester had rung to thank him for tracing a London man and his girl-friend who had stayed at six hotels in Lancashire and walked out without paying their bill at any of them. The job had taken the best part of three days, and it wouldn't exactly make him rich, but all assignments were grist to the mill, and every pound he earned was a pound towards Les's rent. Also it might lead to more work from the same source in the future.

There was one other message. A man's voice said, "My name is Renton." It was an elderly voice, incisive, and with a public school accent, the voice of a man accustomed to giving orders, and to taking it for granted that they would be obeyed. "My wife mentioned your name, Mr. Craig; I understand that you met recently. I would like to come to see you on Monday. Say ten-thirty. If that isn't convenient, give me a ring. My number's Fawchester 54367. Don't leave a message, or say who you are, if I should be out, ring back later. "'Bye."

At least it was to the point, Craig thought. But why should Paula Renton's husband want to see him, and clearly without her knowing? He switched off the machine and took down his old, secondhand copy of *Who's Who.* Lieutenant Colonel Seymour Arthur Gervase Renton MC had been born in 1918, the only son of Robert Stanley Victor Renton DSO MC, and educated at Eton and Trinity College, Cambridge. He had been married twice, but had no children by either wife. There was a list of the companies of which Renton was a director, and the charities of which he was a patron. Several of them were household names. A man of standing then, and very likely wealthy.

Craig put the book back and, going into the outer office, sat down at the desk, took paper and carbon from one of its drawers and started typing the report for the bank. Every minute or so he hit a wrong key, swore and reached out for the Tipp-Ex bottle.

He had almost finished typing his account to go with the report when the phone on the desk in the inner room rang and he went to answer it.

"There's a Colonel Renton to see you," Georgie told him.

"I'll come out," Craig said.

Seymour Renton was a smaller man than he had pictured him, he was no more than five feet eight and slightly built. But while he was nearing seventy, he looked as if he had been fashioned out of whipcord, and his complexion was tanned like old leather. Craig formed the impression of a man who had lived hard, and probably played hard too. There was nothing weak about his handshake, or the look of his shrewd pale blue eyes.

"Craig?" he asked.

"Yes," Craig agreed.

"I rang to make an appointment. As I didn't hear from you I took it the time was all right." The colonel's manner was surprisingly mild and his tone courteous.

"Perfectly," Craig told him.

They went into the inner office and sat down. Craig waited.

"I may as well tell you, I've never had dealings with one of you people before. Never thought I would." Renton stopped and eyed Craig appraisingly.

He might have been ridiculous, Craig reflected, a caricature of a retired regular army colonel. But he wasn't; on the contrary there was something rather impressive about him. His tone was business-like but courteous, and he seemed to imply that his failure to have had dealings with an enquiry agent before was somehow a shortcoming on his part.

The pause became a silence. Now that the preliminaries were over the colonel appeared to be at a loss how to explain why he was there. Perhaps he was beginning to regret having come.

"You said on the phone that Mrs. Renton had mentioned me," Craig prompted him.

"Yes. Just that you were going to take part in something, but it was cancelled when that girl killed herself." With the air of a man speaking on impulse and not much liking what he hears himself saying Renton asked, "Did you and Mrs. Renton talk?"

Craig thought he knew now what this

was all about, and he didn't like it. "Not much" he answered. "I only flew out there on the Friday, I didn't have much to do with any of the party."

"But you did talk to her?"

"Once or twice. We had brunch at the same table on the train."

"How did she seem to you?"

Craig wondered what he was supposed to say. That Renton's wife had struck him as being attractive and pleasant in a superficial way, but that he suspected that under it she was cold and aloof? "In what way?" he asked.

"Did you think she was worried about anything? Upset?"

"I didn't know her well enough to tell. I couldn't judge if the way she was then was how she usually was."

Renton pounced on the half-admission. "So there was something?" he demanded.

Craig stirred restlessly. Any minute now the colonel would ask him if there was another man. That was why he had come to him, a stranger, rather than one of the other members of the Pagets' party who knew Paula much better than he did. Men like Renton would think of enquiry agents only in connection with divorce.

"I got the impression that she had something on her mind," he conceded reluctantly. "Don't misunderstand me, Colonel, but is Mrs. Renton usually reserved?"

The older man's eyes met Craig's squarely. "I dare say some people would say so," he replied. "She doesn't show what she's feeling all the time, if that's what you mean."

"Not quite," Craig told him. "She seemed to me sort of withdrawn. But as I said, I didn't know her well enough to judge. I was probably wrong."

"I don't think you were. I'm worried." It was clear that Renton was telling the truth. "I think it's serious. We've been married over twenty years; I know her pretty well, and I've never seen her like this before."

It occurred to Craig that either the colonel was making a mountain out of a molehill, or Mrs. Renton had changed considerably since she returned home. Yet there had been something. He waited, suppressing the irritation he felt. Renton had no intention of hiring him, all he had come here for was to ask him about his wife's state of mind while she was away.

"I'm sorry, that's all I can tell you," he said. "You'd do better to ask somebody who knows her well."

"No," Renton told him emphatically. "If I went to one of her friends, she would hear about it, and that's the last thing I want. I came here to ask you if you'd noticed anything. You had. Now I want you to find out what it is that's bothering her."

Craig regarded him with astonishment. That possibility hadn't occurred to him. "You may not realise it, Colonel," he said, "but you're asking the impossible."

"I thought it was the sort of work you people did."

"Then you've been watching too much television. Ninety per cent of my work is tracing people other people want to find.

146

Nice tangible people. There's nothing tangible about a worry. I only look for things I can put my hands on if I have to."

"Try."

"No. It's very likely something personal I'd have no way of discovering. Has it occurred to you that she may have learnt she's got some serious illness, and she wants to keep it from you to save you worrying?" Craig remembered something he had overheard in Venice. It was one of Betty Layton's malicious titbits, but had there been a kernel of truth in it? "Or it's possible — " he began.

"That there's another man," the colonel interrupted him. "I know, I'm not a fool. If there is, I'll have to face it and decide what I'm going to do, but I'm as sure as I can be that there isn't. I tell you, we've been married a long time, and I know my wife."

Craig wondered how many other husbands had said that, only to be disillusioned.

"It's something else," Renton insisted. "I've thought about her being ill, it was the first thing I did think of, but I don't think it's the answer either. And if it is . . . " He looked as if he was forcing himself to face that possibility now. "Once she sees I know it will make things easier for her."

"Why not ask her straight out?" Craig suggested. "People are often glad to get secrets off their chests. Especially if they are afraid."

"No!" The colonel spoke more forcefully than ever.

I bet he was a sod to serve under, Craig thought, but at least you'd know where you were with him. People like Renton were bred and trained to command.

The older man looked awkward. "I'm very fond of my wife. Something's bothering her, and for some reason she doesn't want to tell me what it is. I want to put an end to it without making her."

"Even if she really doesn't want you to know?" Craig asked.

"Yes," the colonel said, his jaws closing conclusively over the word.

Suddenly Craig understood: Renton believed his wife was being blackmailed. That put a different complexion on things. Blackmail, or investigating it, *was* his business.

"Has Mrs. Renton received any letters that seemed to upset her?" he enquired. They didn't have to be blackmail threats, he told himself, they could have been poison pen letters.

Renton met his gaze without flinching. His expression gave nothing away. "She gets a great many letters," he replied. "She's on several committees and she does a lot of charity work."

"But, as far as you know, none of them has upset her?"

"No."

"Nor any phone calls?"

"No."

Which meant nothing, or next to nothing. If Mrs. Renton received so many letters, she probably took them off somewhere to open and read, and her husband wouldn't have seen her reaction if one of them contained a threat.

"Had she been married before?" Craig asked.

"No, she was only twenty-four when she married me. I'm twenty years older than she is, but that's never seemed to matter. Even when she was young she was more interested in the sort of life we lead and taking part in local things than in gadding about." Rather gruffly the colonel added, "And I like to think I'm young for my age." His tone suggested that that was something he rarely admitted, even to himself.

"You've no children, have you?" Craig asked.

"No. My first wife was pregnant when she died, and the present Mrs. Renton can't have children." The older man looked irritated, and he stirred restlessly on his chair. "Is all this necessary?"

"It's necessary," Craig told him. "I don't know if it will prove anything." It seemed unlikely that her inability to have children would suddenly have started to trouble Mrs. Renton now when she was forty-eight. Unless her age was the key to the whole business. "Did she know Mary Thornton well?" he asked.

The colonel looked puzzled. "I don't remember the name," he said. "Who is she?"

"The girl who committed suicide on the Orient Express."

"Oh." Renton frowned. "Nasty business. I believe she came to see my wife once. Something to do with a book she was writing about the town."

"Mrs. Renton didn't seem more distressed than you'd expect her to be when she killed herself?"

"No. Why should she? It was a sad thing to happen, but she hardly knew the girl. Anyway, her being worried started before then."

Craig remembered the feeling he had had that morning on the train, that although Paula seemed to be shocked, secretly she was relieved. He had seen Ruth Adamson eyeing her curiously too. But he must have been mistaken, why should she be relieved because a girl she hardly knew had committed suicide?

"When did you first notice anything?" he asked.

"About a month ago," Renton replied. "Maybe a bit more. It's been worse since she got back from Venice."

They eyed each other across the desk, the older man's concern apparent.

"All right," Craig said. "I don't like it, I don't like any job where I don't think there's a hope of getting anywhere, but if you want me to try, that's your business. I'll see what I can do. One thing, though. If I'm going to take it on, I've got to know everything you do. Keep anything back and you'll be wasting my time and your money, because I won't have any chance at all of finding out what you want to know."

"I've told you everything I can." There was no sign that the colonel resented the younger man's tone, and perhaps he understood that he had adopted it deliberately in order to discourage him. "I'll know I've tried," he said quietly.

"We've been married twenty-four years, and we've been very happy. At least, I have, and I've always thought my wife was too. I still think so."

He really loves her, Craig thought. He wondered if he would have acted as the colonel had if Jean was troubled like Paula Renton. Would he have done his utmost to discover what was worrying her, or would he have decided that, if she didn't want to tell him, he had no right to violate her secret? He didn't know. But he could respect the colonel's motives.

"Have you a photograph of Mrs. Renton?" he asked.

"Only a small one I keep in my wallet." Renton looked embarrassed, as if he had been caught out in an unseemly display of sentiment. "Why do you need one? She isn't missing."

"I may have to talk to people who don't know her by name," Craig explained.

The colonel took out his wallet, extracted a small, rather dogeared picture, and handed it to him. From

Paula's clothes it must have been taken at least ten years before, but she had changed remarkably little.

"Is that all?" Renton demanded.

"For the time being."

Craig told the colonel his charges, and the old man nodded. He seemed hardly interested.

When he had gone Craig sat down at his desk again and wondered where he should start. How could he hope to learn what was worrying Paula Renton without talking to her? But the colonel had been insistent that she mustn't know about his enquiries. That didn't make his task more difficult, it made it damned near impossible. But he had promised to try, and if Renton was prepared to pay him when it was almost certain that he would achieve nothing, that was up to him. He could probably afford to do so a lot better than he, Craig, could afford to turn the job down.

Renton appeared to believe that his wife was being blackmailed. On the face of it it seemed unlikely. For one thing, Society had become so tolerant of personal foibles and indiscretions that people were less inclined to pay up to preserve their guilty secrets than they might once have been. Nevertheless they might still do so to preserve a marriage, especially when the husband was as wealthy as Renton probably was, or to protect the feelings of a loved one. Did Paula love her husband as much as he seemed to her?

It was a cockeyed set-up altogether, Craig told himself. Normally in blackmail cases it was the victim who sought help, not a third party, and if this was blackmail, it was extremely unlikely that he would learn anything without Mrs. Renton's cooperation. Which he couldn't have.

Hell! he thought. But one thing, at least, was clear: he would have to go to Fawchester.

7

CRAIG disliked small towns. His ancestry might be Scots, but he was a Londoner by birth and inclination, and he felt out of place in them. Even, at times, a little ill at ease. They were too good to be true with their wide High Streets lined with picturesque old buildings and their air of middle class prosperity. Moreover they possessed subtleties and nuances of which he was dimly aware, but which he didn't understand. There was about them a relaxed formality, an acceptance of a social structure which didn't seem to have changed very much since 1900. People knew each other and their places in the community. It could be disconcerting for a stranger, but, Craig was prepared to admit, it could also be useful to an enquiry. Provided the town didn't close up like a clam.

Fawchester was not much bigger than many villages, it could call itself a town only by reason of the market which had been held in its wide, sloping High Street every Tuesday since the Middle Ages. The market in its turn owed its being to Fawchester's position at the centre of an area of farms and small villages. Once the town had been improbably dignified with the status of an urban district, but the last local government reforms had swept it squalling into the embrace of two larger places, and in the eyes of Whitehall it no longer existed save as part of the District and Council of Lambsdown. Once the hub of a rural community, now it was a dormitory for better off commuters and a refuge for retired professional and Army people.

Craig drove down the High Street slowly, taking in the shops with their modern fronts in eighteenth and nineteenth century plaster, the four banks, five building societies, and six pubs. The church, halfway down on the right-hand side, dominated the street and the bookshop and baker's nestling in its shadow. A few yards farther on was a shabby early Victorian house with a sign 'COUNTY LIBRARY' and its hours of opening beside the door.

Almost opposite the library the Golden Hart Hotel (free house, two stars AA and RAC) stood back from the street behind a small cobbled area. An arch linked it to the next-door building, and Craig waited for a young mother pushing one baby in a pushchair and leading another only slightly older to pass before he drove in under it. The yard beyond had space for about thirty cars. There were only two there now, a nearly new VW and an elderly, rather battered Ford Escort. Craig parked his eight-year-old Dolomite Sprint beside the Escort, took his bag from the back and walked round to the front of the hotel.

Glass panelled swing doors led from the pavement into a lobby with dark wood, vaguely Regency wallpaper, and unobtrusive lighting. The lighting didn't dispel the somnolent atmosphere common to most small country hotels in the dead hours between the bars closing after lunch and their reopening for the evening and the reception desk was unattended. Craig rang the little brass bell, and after a brief wait a dark, rather pretty girl came through a door at the back, smiled and said, "Good afternoon, sir."

"My name's Craig," Craig told her. "I phoned and booked a room for two nights."

"Oh yes, Mr. Craig. It's number twelve."

The girl showed him up a winding flight of stairs to a pleasant, airy room at the front of the hotel, handed him his key, and departed in a gentle waft of perfume. Putting his bag down, Craig crossed to the open window and looked out. Immediately below him was a strip of garden barely three feet wide bright with scarlet and pink geraniums. It was protected from the pavement by a low post and chain fence, and beyond that was the cobbled extension to the street. Craig supposed that the cobbled area was a legacy from the days when the Golden Hart was a coaching inn, although what it could have been used for he had no idea, it was nothing like big enough to have accommodated the market. Now it appeared to serve as an unauthorised parking place, making the turn in under the arch even more difficult than it need have been. Turning away from the window, he slipped off his jacket and ran some hot water into the basin.

When he went downstairs a few minutes later the pretty receptionist was doing something with a thin wad of cards. She smiled brightly at Craig. He smiled back, walked out through the swing doors, and crossed the street to the bookshop near the church. It was small, and appeared to be devoted exclusively to paperbacks, postcards, and slim local guides. The owner, a stout, middle-aged lady with glasses and an eager expression, eyed him hopefully.

Craig bought a large scale map of the town and a 95p guide, and while the woman was putting them into a bag asked, "Do you know a Mrs. Adamson in Fawchester?"

"Ruth Adamson you mean? The author?" The owner had a surprisingly deep voice which seemed to emanate from somewhere behind the ample expanse of mauve cardigan enveloping her bosom.

"Yes," Craig agreed, wondering how many Mrs. Adamsons lived in the town. But perhaps Ruth had a daughter-in-law here.

"Oh yes!"

"Do you happen to know where she lives?"

"Church Cottage. It's just round the corner in Church Street. Turn left outside here and it's only a few yards along."

Craig thanked her and paid for his purchases.

"She'll be at home now; I saw her go past a few minutes ago," the shop's owner told him. "She always writes in the mornings, so you won't be disturbing her."

Lucky Ruth Adamson, Craig thought. It must be a great life being an author,

161

working when you felt like it, with nobody disturbing you. At the same time, wasn't there something slightly odd about somebody sitting at a desk day after day making up stories? Not that there had seemed anything in the least odd about Mrs. Adamson.

Church Cottage was larger than he had expected, a white washed seventeenth century house with lattice windows and a front door opening directly on to the narrow pavement. There was no bell, and he wielded the iron knocker as gently as he could.

Its sound had hardly died away before Ruth opened the door.

"Alan!" she exclaimed. "What a nice surprise! Come in." She led the way into a snug, low-ceilinged room furnished with comfortable old easy chairs and one or two pieces which Craig decided were genuine antiques and probably good. There were bookcases along two of the walls, several pictures and some silver on a mahogany cabinet.

"I had to come to Fawchester," he

explained. "I saw you go by a few minutes ago, and I thought I'd just knock on your door and say hallo. I hope you don't mind."

"Of course not," Ruth assured him. "I'm glad you did. Will you have a cup of tea? I was just going to."

"Thank you. But I didn't mean to be a nuisance."

"You aren't."

Ruth went out of the room, leaving the door open behind her. Craig heard her filling a kettle, then the soft clink of crockery. A cupboard door closed with a gentle thud. Standing up, he walked over to the mahogany cabinet and looked at the silver set out on it. Craig was no expert, but he had been involved in several cases where silver had been stolen, and he had picked up a certain amount of knowledge from people who were. Three of Mrs. Adamson's pieces looked to him like Georgian, and if he was right, they were valuable. There was some nice porcelain inside the cabinet, too. He turned away as Ruth came back into the room.

"It won't be long," she said, perching on the arm of one of the easy chairs, a sturdy figure in her dark blouse and skirt.

"You must miss Mary about the house," Craig remarked disingenuously.

Ruth didn't answer immediately, and it occurred to him that she was too honest to lie easily or to respond with a conventional half-truth.

"The house does seem empty sometimes," she admitted. "But she wasn't here very long, only five months, and I'd been used to living on my own for a good many years before she came. My husband died eleven years ago, and we didn't have any children."

Like the Rentons, Craig thought irrelevantly. But then they were the reason for his being here. "You didn't like Mary much, did you?" he asked quietly.

Ruth gave him a quick, surprised look, and he wondered if the question had angered her, but she answered in her usual calm, matter-of-fact way, "No, not very much, I'm afraid. It wasn't her fault. Not all of it, anyway. I think I've become rather intolerant living alone, and people irritate me more than they should do. This house is too big for one person, especially when they're not as young as they were, and I wanted somebody to share it, but when Mary came I resented her being here. I feel rather guilty about that now, as if, if I'd liked her more and been more friendly, she might not have done what she did."

"You don't really believe that, do you?" Craig asked.

"No, I know it isn't true. It's just that sometimes . . ." With a muttered, "Excuse me," Ruth stood up and went out to the kitchen.

Craig wondered if she had welcomed the excuse to break off their conversation then.

It was two or three minutes before she returned carrying a tray loaded with tea things and a chocolate cake. Putting the tray down on a small table between them, she busied herself pouring out.

"Milk and sugar?" she asked.

"Milk but no sugar, please," Craig told her. "Do you think Mary jumped into the canal to draw attention to herself?"

Ruth looked at him over the cup she was holding out. "No," she answered. "It's possible, I suppose, but . . . I don't know. I just can't believe she would. She was intelligent, she'd have realised how dangerous it was, and I don't think she'd have risked losing her glasses; she was nearly blind without them." Ruth paused. "All the same, looking back, she must have been in a terrible state, and when somebody's like that they don't think logically. Will you have some cake? It's home-made, I'm afraid. I have a dreadful weakness for anything chocolate, and it's so difficult to buy good cakes here."

"Thank you." Ruth cut him a generous slice of the cake and Craig took it. Again he suspected that she was deliberately avoiding talking about Mary. Many women would have been only too ready to tell him all they knew about her, he thought. Did Ruth's reticence stem from her sense of what was right and in good taste, or had she some other reason for side-stepping the subject? "That morning on the train when I told you what had happened, you said, *'Mary?* You do mean Mary?' as if you'd almost been expecting somebody else to die," he said.

"No!" Ruth refuted it forcefully.

"I'm sorry," Craig apologised. "I don't mean you really expected it, just that it sounded as if you did."

"Isn't that the same thing? No, perhaps it isn't." Ruth looked at Craig as if he had surprised her again and she had to revise her opinion of him in some way. "I don't see any reason why I shouldn't tell you. Betty had been saying some outrageous things about other people all the time we were out there, and one of the others remarked that if she didn't look out, somebody would shut her up once and for all. She didn't mean it, it was just one of those silly things people say, but when you told me what had happened I was still half asleep, and I remembered it."

For once Ruth was being less than truthful, Craig told himself: she hadn't been half asleep. All the same, he believed what she had told him about Betty. Anyway, he wasn't very interested in Mary Thornton, he had only used her as cover for his real purpose in calling.

"I saw Mrs. Renton in the street just now," he remarked casually.

"Oh?" Ruth sounded surprised, but her head was bent over the tray so that he couldn't see her face. "I thought she was still away. I saw her on Friday and she said she was going up to Yorkshire for two or three days, so she wouldn't be able to take the chair at the church council meeting this evening. I told her I'd been to Sheffield for Mary's funeral, and that I'd seen Mary's brother there. He was her only close relative, and he asked if he could leave her things here for a fortnight because he was going on holiday. There isn't much, she always said she hadn't anything valuable, and I told him of course he could."

"It can't have been Mrs. Renton then," Craigh said lightly. "Whoever it was was some way off. How did she seem when you saw her?"

"Just as usual. Why?"

"I'd never met her before that day in Venice, but she didn't strike me as being what you'd call cheerful."

"Oh?" Ruth said.

"I thought she was aloof. You know, the grand lady. But p'raps that's the way she always is."

"I wouldn't say so. She isn't very demonstrative, but she's perfectly friendly, and she certainly isn't a snob. I think she enjoys life, and people like her."

"Maybe she was just worried about something," Craig suggested.

"I don't know." As if speaking to herself, Ruth added, "She's changed lately."

It was Craig's turn to say, "Oh?"

Ruth hesitated, regretting having said

so much. Now if she only told him, "Nothing, it wasn't anything," he wouldn't believe her. Alan Craig, she was sure, was no fool.

"While we were in Venice she seemed upset, as if she had something on her mind, and I wondered if she wasn't well," she explained. "But then when we were chatting one day she said how lucky she was to have such good health, so I must have been wrong." Craig might be a pleasant young man, but he was almost a stranger, Ruth thought. She shouldn't be discussing Paula with him. "What brings you to Fawchester?" she enquired.

"A dull routine job," Craig answered easily. "You may not believe it, but most of my work's tracing people who don't pay their bills."

"I can't imagine Paula welshing on a debt," Ruth commented.

Craig smiled. "Neither can I."

"I wondered why you were so interested in her."

"Did I seem to be?"

170

"You did rather." Ruth finished her cake and put down her plate. "Oh well," she said more briskly, "if anything's bothering her it's her affair, and I'm sure she'll work things out for herself. She's far too sensible to do anything silly, and if there is anything in what — " She stopped abruptly.

Craig was far too experienced to prompt her, and he waited patiently, but all she said was, "Will you have another piece of cake?"

"No, thank you. That was great." Craig decided that he had better give Ruth a more satisfactory explanation for his being in Fawchester than he had done so far. "Do you know anybody called Applegarth?" he asked.

"Old Lionel?" There was no mistaking Ruth's amusement. "I've known him for over twenty years. Don't say he's one of your defaulters."

Craig cursed his luck. Applegarth had seemed as unlikely a name to encounter in Fawchester as any he could think of on the spur of the moment, and he had been wrong. "Not Lionel, no," he said.

"The only other Applegarth in Fawchester is Florrie, Lionel's wife, and she's over eighty like him." Ruth smiled. "Unless it's somebody in one of the new houses in Highfields." Seeing Craig's expression, she explained, "It's that new estate off London Road."

"Perhaps it is," Craig agreed. "Applegarth is the name I was given."

"Oh well, we all make mistakes," Ruth observed a little enigmatically.

Craig told himself that it was time he left, he wouldn't learn any more here. "I mustn't take up any more of your time," he said, standing up. "Thank you very much for tea."

"It was nice of you to call," Ruth told him. She led the way out to the hall. "This is the part of the house I kept for myself, there's another staircase at the back goes up to the rooms Mary had. They used to be a granny flat that we had made for my mother-in-law." She opened the front door. "Goodbye, Alan. I do hope you haven't had a wasted journey."

"So do I," Craig agreed.

And where did he go from here? he asked himself as he walked back along Church Street. Colonel Renton had stipulated that on no account must his wife learn that he was asking questions about her, but how could he avoid that in a close little community like Fawchester?

He was pretty sure that Ruth Adamson had seen through his feeble attempt at subterfuge; she was a friend of Mrs. Renton's, and it was quite on the cards that she would mention his visit the next time they met. It would be the same whoever he talked to. They might not tell Mrs. Renton themselves, but they would tell somebody, and it would get back to her eventually. Most likely embellished. Small towns were as bad as villages, he thought bitterly.

All the same, his call hadn't been entirely wasted. Mrs. Adamson had been going to say something when she changed her mind and stopped abruptly. Something that somebody had said about

Paula Renton? When he had walked into the bar at the Michele with her and Leila that night Betty Layton had been hinting that there was some sort of relationship between Mrs. Renton and Clive Winters. Craig doubted if you could believe half of what Betty said, but the next evening on the Orient Express Winters had addressed Mrs. Renton as 'Paula' in a way that suggested they knew each other well, and she, evidently annoyed, had snubbed him.

At the time Craig had dismissed the snub as the reaction of a woman over-conscious of her social status to a younger man's familiarity. It was one of the factors which had contributed to his opinion of her. But perhaps he was wrong, and she had seen Winters' manner as dangerously indiscreet. On the face of it, an affair between Winters and the cool, aloof Mrs. Renton seemed unlikely, but what had likelihood to do with such things?

At least he had settled one question, Craig thought: Paula Renton wasn't ill.

At the end of Church Street he turned right and walked down the High Street towards the fork in the road at the bottom of the hill. A hundred yards along he came to a bright looking double fronted shop with a sign 'PAGET TRAVEL' over the door. Through one window he could see Norma Paget and a young assistant dealing with two customers. Another girl was on the phone. Craig walked on without stopping, he would much prefer neither Norma nor her husband to know that he was in Fawchester.

Just before the fork a large red brick building stood well back from the street behind an asphalted yard. There was no sign of life in the yard, but three lorries and several cars were parked against the wall at one side. The original building was late-Victorian and resembled a large mill, but a modern extension had been built on to one side of it, and there were a number of outbuildings. A familiar strong, sweet scent came from them, and Craig didn't need the iron sign over the entrance to tell him that this was the Fawchester brewery. He wondered if Winters was there now.

Crossing the street, he walked back up the hill on the other side. Sue, the receptionist, was still at her desk, busy with the cards and a big ledger. Computerisation, apparently, hadn't yet reached the Golden Hart. Craig went up to his room, tossed the bag containing the map and guide he had bought on to the bed and sat down in the only chair.

Colonel Renton had said that he was as sure as he could be that his wife hadn't a lover. Had he been a bit too sure about it? It was conceivable that that was exactly what he secretly suspected, but that he wasn't prepared to admit it, even to himself. If so, he had hired him either to prove his fears groundless, or to confirm them almost by accident, as it were, while he was looking for something else. You never knew with people like the colonel, they were never wholly open and frank with you. Like another 99.9 per cent of the population, they told you only what they wanted you to know.

A woman like Mrs. Renton, proud, reserved, rather fastidious, and very conscious of her position in the district, if she became involved in an affair with another man, might well be torn between infatuation and guilt. Craig hadn't seen much of her, but he had noticed a worried, half-fearful expression on her attractive face more than once. And each time she had been looking at Winters. Was it the look of a woman many years older than her lover and unsure of him?

Unfolding his map, Craig spread it out on the bed. Fawchester Court was marked a mile to the south of the town. Living in a house that size, the Rentons must have some sort of staff, he thought, and servants were traditionally the richest source of information about their employers. But he couldn't go there to see them, it would be too risky. Renton would bitterly resent his questioning his staff about their mistress, and Paula might return at any time and find him there. He would have to find out if any of the staff frequented a pub in the town.

Craig had gone to see Ruth Adamson because she seemed to offer his best hope of learning anything about Paula Renton; they were friendly, and Mrs. Adamson was shrewd. It would have helped if he could have explained straight out why he was there, but the colonel had ruled that out. As it was, he had known he was taking a risk because she knew his job, but it had seemed worth it. Anyway, she was the only lead he had. Now he wasn't sure that it had been worth it. If the colonel learnt that he'd talked to her about his wife, he would be off the case before he had time to say 'Winters,' and he'd be lucky if he was paid even his expenses. He had better come up with something fast, before Renton found out.

There was a telephone on the bedside table and a directory on the shelf. Craig looked up a number and dialled it.

"Fawchester Brewery," a woman's voice said.

"Can I speak to Mr. Winters, please?" Craig asked.

"I'm sorry, Mr. Winters is away."

"Oh. Do you know when he'll be back?"

"Not for another day or two. Can anybody else help?"

"Not really. I have to get in touch with him quickly, his brother-in-law's been killed in a car crash." Brother-in-law was safer than brother or sister, Craig thought. He just hoped that Winters wasn't an only child and the telephonist knew it.

"Oh no!" she exclaimed, her tone charged with sympathy. "Look, I'll put you through to Miss Evans, his secretary. She may know where he is. What name shall I tell her?"

"Godbolt," Craig said. "I'm the next-door neighbour."

"Just a minute please, Mr. Godbolt."

Craig waited. In less than a minute another woman's voice said, "Mr.

Godbolt? I'm sorry to keep you waiting. Mr. Winters is in London on business. He's staying at the Crossland Hotel in Kensington."

"Thank you very much," Craig said. He felt a pang of guilt; he had never become completely reconciled to lying in order to use people. "I'll ring him there. I'm very grateful."

"Not at all," the girl told him. "Please tell Mr. Winters that if there's anything we can do . . ."

"I will," Craig promised. "Goodbye."

He put down the phone. It wasn't much, and it might lead nowhere, but at least it was a start.

8

IT might be only coincidence, of course; Mrs. Renton had told Ruth Adamson that she was going to Yorkshire.

Craig rummaged in his bag for the notepaper and envelopes he kept there and sat down to write to a fellow enquiry agent in London. When he had finished the letter he put it in an envelope with the photograph the colonel had given him and went out to post it. With any luck he would get a call from Dave Smith by tomorrow evening.

Returning to his room, Craig stretched out on his back on the bed and considered what he knew. If Paula Renton was having an affair with Winters and had lied about going to Yorkshire, that might explain her anxiety. But what if she wasn't? On the face of it she had everything a woman could want, except, perhaps, children. She had a loving husband who happened also to he wealthy, looks, a fine home, and good health. But Craig knew they weren't necessarily enough. That she hadn't confided in her husband suggested either a guilty secret or a wish to protect him from knowledge which would hurt him. Apparently it wasn't anything to do with her own health, but what about his? He looked fit enough, it was true, but appearances weren't always a reliable guide, and he was nearly seventy. Craig made a mental note to find out whether the colonel had seen a doctor lately.

All the same, he didn't think that that was the answer. He was fairly sure that Renton suspected that his wife was being blackmailed, and it remained a distinct possibility. But how did you find out whether somebody was being blackmailed if they wouldn't admit it? If he had been free to talk to Mrs. Renton, he might have been able to persuade her to tell him — or, at least, he might have known from her manner whether she was or not — but the colonel had vetoed that. The colonel had vetoed everything. It was almost as if while anxious to give the impression that he was doing all he could to discover what was troubling his wife, in reality he was determined to prevent its coming out.

Craig didn't like where that train of thought was taking him.

One way of checking on possible blackmail was to examine the supposed victim's bank account. He hadn't suggested it before, because he had known that the colonel would resist the idea, but now he couldn't see any alternative. Picking up the phone, he dialled the number Renton had given him.

The colonel answered himself, and Craig guessed that it was a private line to Renton's study. "Craig," he said. "Are you alone?"

"Yes." Renton couldn't quite suppress his eagerness. "Have you found out anything?"

"Give me time!" Craig protested. "I

only got here a couple of hours ago. I need to see your wife's bank statements, Colonel. Can you get hold of the last four or five months'?"

"No!" Renton sounded outraged.

It was no more than Craig had expected, but that didn't do anything to ease his frustration. "Look," he said roughly, "you hire me to do a job, then you put every obstacle in my way you can. You won't let me talk to her, you won't have anybody know what I'm supposed to be doing, and now you won't get her statements. Don't you want me to find out anything, Colonel?"

Renton controlled his anger with difficulty. He wasn't used to being spoken to in that way, but he had been a good officer, and now he was a successful administrator, and he knew that there was nothing to be gained by indulging in a slanging match with Craig. "If you aren't prepared to accept my conditions, say so and I'll find somebody who is," he said harshly.

"You tie his hands like you've tied

mine, and you'll be lucky to get anybody honest to work for you," Craig told him. He had set out to anger the colonel, because if Renton was angry enough he just might agree to what Craig wanted, if only to shut him up, but he had failed. Either the old man had nothing to hide, or he was more subtle than Craig had believed. More devious, too.

There was a brief silence.

"Very well, I'll see what I can do," Renton agreed coldly.

"Thank you," Craig said in a more conciliatory tone. "Remember, it's to help her."

"You think I'm likely to forget? Where can I get in touch with you?"

"The Golden Hart. I'll be here for the next day or two."

"Very well," Renton said again. There was a click as he put down his phone.

Goodbye to you too, Craig thought. But he had achieved something, even if it wasn't very much; it looked as if the colonel was prepared to bury his scruples and try to get hold of his wife's statements. And if they revealed nothing?

Eliminate adultery, serious illness, and blackmail, and what was left? Someone close to her in trouble of some kind? If it were that, and her relationship with her husband was all that it was supposed to be, surely she would have told him? Another possibility occurred to Craig, was she about to be prosecuted for something? Say, drunken or dangerous driving? But again, surely she would have confided in the colonel? He would know soon enough, in any case. Once the case came to court it would be reported in the papers.

She might not know that. Or, if she did, be clinging desperately to the hope that somehow he would never find out. For people like the Rentons, whatever the sentence, the shame and humiliation of conviction would be infinitely harder to bear than for some of the offenders Craig had known in the old days. They would care about a lot more than losing a driving licence for a year or two.

It would be the same if she had committed some other offence. It was hard to imagine Mrs. Renton shoplifting, but so it was hard to imagine many of the respectable middle-class women who were convicted every year helping themselves to things in shops for which they could afford to pay but didn't. People said it was an illness, or a cry for help. Perhaps they were right. If so, and that was what she had done, Paula Renton needed help fast.

But it was more likely that she was simply bored and no longer cared for her husband. A woman like her might well try to hide it from him, feel guilty, and become depressed.

With evening it had become a good deal cooler, and somebody had lit a log fire in the bar. When Craig walked in at twenty past six it was blazing cheerfully with no one to enjoy it but a large black Labrador stretched out as close to the hearth as it could get without burning itself. As he went up to the bar it raised its head and watched him with brown, soulful eyes.

The Golden Hart prided itself on its range of beers, and there was an impressive row of pump handles on the bar. Craig remembered Winters' telling him that the local bitter wasn't a bad beer, and when Sue, acting as barmaid until the regular girl came on duty, came to serve him he asked her for a pint of Crown. She took down a glass from the shelf behind her and drew the beer while Craig watched appreciatively; working the pump handle stretched her blouse taut across her nicely curved figure.

The beer looked all right, he thought. Just enough head, neither too lively nor too flat, nice and clear, and the right temperature. The cellarman at the Golden Hart knew his job.

"Will you have something?" he asked Sue.

"Thank you," she said. "May I have an orange juice?"

Mary Thornton had had a passion for orange juice, Craig thought. In the end it, or what she had taken in it, had killed her.

"Do you know Clive Winters?" he asked.

"Clive?" She smiled in a way which suggested that she knew him very well. "He's the sales manager at the brewery, he's always in here." She raised her glass. "Cheers."

"Cheers," Craig said. He paid for their drinks and sipped his beer. Winters had been too modest, it was as good as any he had tasted for a long time. "We were on the same trip a few weeks ago," he explained. "He's one for the girls, isn't he?"

This time Sue laughed aloud, showing small, even teeth very white against her bright red lips. "You can say that again," she agreed.

"And older women?" Craig suggested.

"I wouldn't know about that."

Two men came in together. Sue greeted them by name and went along the bar to serve them. Other customers followed. Clearly there wouldn't be another opportunity for a quiet word with her for some time, and Craig took his beer and evening paper over to a chair near the fire. The Labrador reluctantly moved its head a couple of inches to make room for him.

Soon afterwards the regular barmaid took over, and Sue disappeared. Craig finished reading his paper, and shortly after seven went in to dinner. By then the bar was busy.

He had no doubt who would be his most willing source of information, true or false, in Fawchester: Betty Layton. But they had hardly spoken to each other in Venice, or on the Orient Express, and he could think of no plausible excuse for calling on her now. Betty, he suspected, was like many other gossips, much quicker than you might expect when it came to nosing out a breath of scandal. If he went to see her, asking about people who lived here, she would immediately put two and two together. She might make the answer thirty-seven, but put them together she assuredly would, and it would soon be all over the town that he was here asking questions. He would have to make do with less obvious sources.

Sue had agreed that Clive Winters was one for the girls; had Mrs. Renton discovered that? If she had, it might account for the looks Craig had seen her giving him. Possibly they had quarrelled about his attentions to other women, and that was why she had snubbed him when he offered to buy her a drink on the train.

Craig lingered over dinner. There wasn't much for a solitary stranger to do in Fawchester after eight o'clock except drink in one or other of the ten pubs, or pick up one of the teenage girls who hung about in twos and threes in the High Street, giggling noisily and wondering what would happen to them. Neither alternative appealed to him, and at half past eight he went up to his room and watched television for a while.

But he was restless and out of sorts with the world. If Colonel Renton wanted to know what was the matter with his wife, why didn't he ask her? She might even tell him. If she didn't, then would be the time for him to employ an enquiry agent — without constraints which made the job virtually impossible.

But that, Craig knew, was only part of the trouble. It was more than eighteen months since Jean died, and sometimes it seemed she had belonged to a different life. Under the pressures of the present the past, and with it his sense of loss, was fading, only to return, sharp and poignant, when he was alone and in low spirits as he was now. He picked up the copy of *A Brief Guide to Fawchester* he had bought that afternoon, wondering why he had bothered with it. Mrs. Renton's problem, whatever it was, was very much of today, and a history wouldn't help him to solve it. But he hadn't anything else to read, and he started turning the pages.

There was a good deal about the house which had stood on the site of Fawchester Court before William

Renton demolished it and built his mansion late in the 1600s, and about the first generations of the family to live in the new house, but little about their successors. The Rentons, it seemed, had settled for the obscurity of rural life.

Craig told himself that it wasn't past Rentons who concerned him, it was the latest woman to marry into the family. She couldn't be the first of the line to take a lover.

Ruth woke feeling as if she had hardly slept, although it was a long time since she had come to bed. It was very dark. Beside her the luminous hands of the clock on the little cabinet pointed to ten minutes past three. Pulling herself into a half-sitting position, she drank a little water from the glass she always put on the cabinet last thing and settled down again, hoping she would drop off quickly.

But sleep eluded her. Her brain was too active, and although she tried to make her mind a blank, she couldn't stop herself turning things over in her mind. Craig's visit had disturbed her. It was only too obvious that his story about coming to Fawchester to see a man named Applegarth and thinking that he would look her up while he was here was only half true, if that. Applegarth himself was an invention, Craig had plucked the name out of the air. It was possible that he had done so to protect a real debtor, but Ruth didn't think so. All that had been a blind. He had come to Fawchester on a job, so much she believed, and he had called on her because he hoped that she would provide him with information. Information about one of two people, Mary and Paula Renton.

It was natural that he should talk about Mary, but why should he be interested in Paula? The answer seemed to Ruth to be horribly obvious, he was a private enquiry agent, a detective, and didn't a lot of their work consist of obtaining evidence for divorce suits? She liked Alan Craig, but now she felt only resentment. It was his job, but he had sought to involve her in something which might harm someone she liked. His visit had been an intrusion.

Leila hadn't known he was coming, and he hadn't been to see her. Which seemed to confirm that his interest was in Paula.

Ruth told herself that her being concerned would do no good, she couldn't change anything, and she turned on to her other side. But it made no difference, sleep still didn't come. Plotting her new book was going badly. Before she went to Venice the basic theme had appealed to her, now it seemed not only terribly contrived, but uninteresting too. Moreover her resolution not to use Francesca any more, far from increasing her confidence and giving her a sense of freedom, had made her unsure of herself. Francesca had been in her last nine books and writing one without her was like making a complicated dish without an important ingredient. It was ridiculous, but she had come to rely on the wretched woman as a prop. Was Leila right, and her most loyal readers would mind? It would be absurd if they did, it would mean that they thought more of Francesca than they did of her stories, but readers did like the same principal character to reappear in each new book. American readers as well as British. Probably German, Japanese, Swedish, French, Dutch, and Italian readers too. She couldn't afford to upset them and lose sales. Nor did she want to, it was a matter of pride as much as money.

All the same, she wouldn't change her mind now. She needed a break from Francesca, and she was still convinced that she would be a better writer for it. Hadn't her last book been a little facile? Even Harry, who was always kind in his reviews, had hinted as much. Perhaps after two or three more books she would use Francesca again, but not yet.

Ruth's thoughts turned to Mary. What had driven her to kill herself? She must have been desperately unhappy. Why hadn't they seen it? Her especially. It was dreadful to know that you had failed someone so badly. Ruth tossed restlessly, longing for sleep, and after a while she dozed.

A sound roused her. There were always noises in an old house at night, but this wasn't like the usual creaks and groans, it was more like somebody bumping into something solid, not loud, but quite distinct. And it had come from inside the house.

She couldn't have imagined it, could she? Half asleep as she was? No, she was sure she hadn't. She lay still, her ears straining for any new sound and her heart pounding.

A floorboard creaked. For another second Ruth hesitated. She was afraid, but more she was angry. There were treasured things downstairs, things which she and Don had collected together, she couldn't just cower here under the bedclothes, and do nothing to save them. Pushing back the duvet, she slid out of bed and put on her dressing gown, fumbling for the sleeves. The ebony-backed hairbrush her mother had given her when she was a girl was on the dressing table. She groped for it in the dark, felt her hand close over it, and picked it up. It had always felt heavy before, now it seemed a punily inadequate weapon. But it was all she had.

Out on the landing the darkness was even more intense. Ruth paused, listening. Surely that was a footstep? Darkness played strange tricks with one's sense of direction, but she was almost certain that it had come from the back of the house. Somebody was in the granny flat.

Her heart thudding against her ribs, Ruth crept down the stairs, feeling her way with her left hand on the banister rail, her feet groping for the edge of each step. She was thankful that concentrating on the stairs saved her from thinking too much about anything else.

When she reached the bottom she stopped again. There was no sound now. The silence seemed charged with menace, as if unseen watchers were lurking there.

Then she heard it again, unmistakable now that she was nearer, a light footstep on a board almost over her head. She made herself edge forward along the passage which led to the back stairs. She had written more than once about cold fingers of fear touching her characters' spines without ever experiencing it herself. Now she knew what it was like. Every nerve in her body was stretched taut.

She stubbed a toe against something hard. The sudden pain brought a little moan to her lips, and she stifled it just in time. She had reached the foot of the back stairs. Awkwardly she began feeling her way up them.

As she did so a light was switched on. It was only a torch, and it was some way off, but Ruth's eyes had become accustomed to the darkness, and for a moment she was blinded. When she could see again she realised that the light was at the far end of the landing. And it was coming towards her.

For a moment panic threatened to overwhelm Ruth. What if this wasn't an ordinary burglar? One read of such ghastly incidents nowadays, torture and violence, even against the very old. And rape. Oh, dear God! She wanted to turn and flee. But that was impossible. It was still dark here, and the stairs were steep and narrow. Take hold of yourself, she thought.

The light was coming nearer every second. Gritting her teeth, she forced herself on.

She was nearly halfway up when the intruder reached the top of the stairs. The light shone on her face. Then for a second the torch wavered and Ruth saw the face behind it.

In an instant of appalled recognition, "You!" she gasped.

On his way down to breakfast Craig paused in the lobby to pick up the *Independent* he had ordered last night.

The only other occupants of the dining room were two obvious sales reps and a middle-aged couple. Craig sat down at the table he had occupied for dinner, and when the waitress came asked for "orange juice and the lot." At home he usually made do with toast or cereal and coffee, but here he was on expenses, and he saw no reason why they shouldn't include a proper breakfast.

"Bacon, egg, sausage, tomato, mushrooms, fried bread," the waitress intoned, scribbling laboriously on her pad. "Do you want your eggs scrambled or fried, dear?"

"Scrambled, please," Craig told her. "And toast and coffee."

She departed and he opened his paper. But this morning even the sports pages lacked interest, the cricket season had finally died its usual lingering death, and the football season was still too young to provide much in the way of drama. There was no major golf to report on Tuesdays, the tennis circuit was in the doldrums, and Craig had never been interested in racing or rugby. When the waitress returned with his orange juice he sipped it, wishing that it hadn't reminded him again of Mary Thornton. He should have asked for grapefruit juice instead.

The reps left one at a time, followed by the couple. Craig finished his breakfast and went out to the lobby. There was no one at the reception desk, but a door marked 'PRIVATE' was open wide enough for him to see into a small office where a man was poring over some papers with the air of one to whom paperwork does not come easily.

Craig tapped on the door and the man looked up.

"Can I help you, sir?" he asked, standing up and coming round from behind his desk.

"I wondered if there was a local paper here," Craig explained.

"Yes, sir, the *Chronicle*. It comes out on Fridays."

"Is the office in Fawchester?"

"Yes. It's down the bottom of the High Street on the left-hand side, the printers Holgates."

"Thank you," Craig said.

He walked out through the swing doors to the street. It was a grey, joyless morning with an autumnal chill in the air and a desultory rain fell in a bored way, pitting the surface of the puddles in the gutters with tiny craters. Across the street a group of people had gathered on the pavement and two cars were parked outside the bookshop. One of them was a police car, and Craig supposed that either the bookshop or the baker's next door had been burgled during the night.

He started down the hill. He hated carrying umbrellas, some youthful prejudice had left him with an ingrained belief that they were effeminate, but he had left his raincoat in his car when he arrived yesterday and he could have used one now. The rain might be light, but it was persistent, and by the time he had covered a couple of hundred yards his thin jacket was distinctly damp. He couldn't be bothered to go back for his coat, and he walked on, cursing silently.

He found the printers without difficulty, a gloomy double fronted shop with faded brown paint, old posters in the windows, and a flat roofed extension built on to the rear. The girl behind the counter looked slovenly and not very bright. When Craig asked her if they kept back numbers of the *Chronicle* she said that she would have to ask Mr. Gracie.

"Mr. Gracie?" Craig repeated.

"'E's the owner." The girl slid off her stool and disappeared through a door at the back of the shop.

Mr. Gracie, when he appeared, turned out to be a small, wispy man of about seventy with pinched features to match his voice which sounded as if it had been filtered through rusty iron filings. He conceded that he did have back numbers of the paper. "Going right back to the first issue in 1863," he declared proudly.

Craig asked if he could look at the most recent ones.

A mercenary gleam came into the old man's eye. "We don't often get asked," he said cunningly. "There'd have to be a charge."

"What for?" Craig had seen the gleam. "I've never had to pay anywhere before."

"If you want to see them, you'll have to pay," Gracie told him irritably. "That's how we work here. Why do you want to look at them?"

"That's my business," Craig told him. "I pay, I don't have to explain. How much?"

The printer was clearly torn between greed and annoyance; he wasn't used to being spoken to like that, and the girl Rosie was listening. But greed won. "Five pounds," he said.

You thieving old basket, Craig thought. He felt like laughing aloud, but taking out his wallet he extracted a five pound note and held it out.

Gracie eyed it. "How far back do you want to go?" he demanded.

"Six months."

"Six months! I thought you meant two or three weeks. I'll have to charge more for that. It means a lot of work lifting those heavy binders up and down, and I'm not as young as I was. It'll be ten pounds."

"No." Craig opened his wallet again. The five pound note hovered over it.

"All right," Gracie agreed crossly. "I'll make an exception for you." Reaching out, he almost snatched the note from Craig's fingers.

Craig grinned. He had saved his client a fiver. Not that Renton would know, or, possibly, care greatly if he did. And, to be honest, his object hadn't been to save the colonel five pounds he could easily afford; he didn't like being twisted by mean minded, grasping little sods like the printer.

"You'd better come through," Gracie grumbled.

The files were housed in a long, dusty room which Craig guessed comprised part of the single storey extension. The air was heavy with the musty odour of old newsprint and through the thin wall down the left-hand side came the hum and clatter of ancient printing machines.

"They're along there," Gracie said. "They start at this end and run round the top shelf, then work down. Six months ago'll be on the bottom shelf at the far end on the other side, I should think." He showed no sign of moving from where he was standing just inside the door.

"Five pounds," Craig reminded him. "You said it was heavy work lifting those binders."

"You don't expect me to lift them, a strapping young fellow like you?" The printer sounded outraged.

"What would you have done for ten pounds?" Craig wanted to know. "The same?"

Gracie eyed him with obvious dislike. "Let Rosie know when you've finished," he said, and, turning, he went out.

Craig set to work. He soon found the binders he wanted, and for the next forty minutes he read through them diligently. By the time he had finished last Friday's issue he knew a good deal more about the Rentons' social and charitable activities, but nothing which explained Paula's distress. He hadn't expected anything else. If she wouldn't confide in her husband, it was hardly likely that he would find the cause anywhere as public as the columns of the local paper.

He had also come across several items of interest only because he knew the people involved. For instance, six months ago a brief paragraph had reported Clive Winters' appointment as sales manager of the brewery company, and there were four references to Ruth Adamson, invariably described as 'the well known Fawchester author.' Three issues had carried an advertisement for Paget Travel's trip to 'See the glories of Venice and experience the thrill of Murder on the Orient Express'. Six weeks ago Michael Paget had won the golf club's monthly medal competition, and in August his wife had talked to the townswomen's guild about winter holidays, while Betty Layton had been runner-up in a bank holiday tennis tournament. None of them was relevant to Craig's quest.

He closed the last binder, returned it to its shelf, and went to let the girl Rosie know that he had finished. She didn't seem very interested.

It had stopped raining and patches of blue sky showed between the clouds as Craig walked up the hill. The same two cars were still outside the bookshop, and farther up the street two more police cars and a dark blue van were parked by the kerb. Near them a small crowd was staring at something Craig couldn't see. He turned into the hotel.

Sue was standing just inside the doors gazing out.

"What's the fuss about?" Craig enquired.

"Haven't you heard?" Sue was torn between horror and excitement. "It's Mrs. Adamson, the author. She's been murdered."

9

DETECTIVE Chief Inspector Raymond Franklin was lean, dark, and, at thirty-seven, still ambitious. He knew that this case could be his big break; Ruth Adamson had been well-known. Solve it quickly and it would look good on his record, bungle it and he might never live it down. So far luck had been on his side; if the super hadn't been on leave he would have taken charge, and Franklin would have been left at divisional HQ to deal with the usual ragbag of routine cases. But he was, and Franklin meant to make the most of his chance.

None of which stood in the way of his genuine sorrow when he saw Ruth Adamson's body lying huddled on the stairs in her house. He hated violent crime, particularly when the victim was elderly or old.

That had been several hours ago, now "What'll you have, Brian?" he enquired, entering the bar at the Golden Hart with Detective Sergeant Salisbury.

"A pint of the local poison, please, guv."

"What do you want to eat?"

Salisbury grinned. "You didn't appreciate it the last time I had cheese and onion rolls," he said.

Franklin looked disgusted. "You're damn right I didn't. God knows where they got those onions, they nearly took the roof off."

"Beef then, please, guv."

The barmaid was waiting expectantly. "Two pints of Crown and two rounds of beef sandwiches, please, love," Franklin told her.

She drew their beer, then went to give the kitchen the order for the sandwiches.

"Cheers," Franklin said. "I used to come in here a lot when I lived in Fawchester. George Musson had it in those days. Awkward old devil he was." He looked round, taking in the changes made since then and weighing them in the scales of his approval. On the whole, he thought, they were an improvement.

"Yes, sir?" Salisbury said politely. He wasn't very interested in older men's reminiscences, but he had learnt not to let it show.

"Yes, well . . . " Franklin, no fool, understood.

It was only a little past midday and there was only one other customer in the bar, an elderly man in a check sports jacket sitting in a corner with a whisky in the glass in front of him and a newspaper sticking out of his pocket. Franklin noted his purplish complexion and watery eye and put him down as a regular. Old men like him were often the first into bars at lunch-times. Many of them had nowhere to go but lonely rooms, poor devils. He thanked God he would never be like them.

A younger man came in, and Franklin stared at him. "What the hell's he doing here?" he muttered half to himself.

Salisbury regarded his boss curiously.

"Who is he, guv?" he asked.

"His name's Craig," Franklin told him. "He's the private fellow who worked with us on that Jordan business. He was staying in the house when Jordan was shot. Now he's here."

Salisbury had heard stories about the Jordan case, and he watched with interest as Craig walked up to the bar and ordered a pint of Crown and a round of beef sandwiches. He hadn't met many private enquiry agents, and most of those he had had been at least middle-aged and shabby. Craig was neither.

"He's ex-Met," Franklin volunteered. "A d/s."

"Why did he get out?"

"Something about a super covering up for a sergeant Craig said was bent. He wouldn't keep quiet about it, so they eased him out. The super retired early on health grounds a few months ago."

"Interesting," Salisbury said.

"Bob Granger hadn't any use for private men as a rule, but he and Craig got on all right." Franklin smiled at some memory. "Once they understood each other."

Craig had paid for his beer and as he turned, picking a table, he saw Franklin. Their eyes met, and for a moment they gazed at each other, watchful as two beasts sizing up their rivals before they fought.

"Hallo, Franklin," Craig said.

The inspector nodded. "Come and join us."

Craig guessed that Franklin didn't want his company, he wanted to know what he was doing here, and he hesitated just long enough for it to be noticeable before he walked over and sat down.

"I didn't think about your being on this one," he remarked.

"The super's on leave," Franklin said.

"Oh. I heard they made you up when Granger went. Congratulations."

"Thanks." Franklin indicated his companion. "D/s Brian Salisbury, Alan Craig. How's life?"

"Not bad," Craig said. He drank some of his beer. "I hear her head had been smashed in. Who found her?"

"The milkman. When he got there just before half-eight the curtains were still drawn and there were no lights showing. She was always up when he came, and he wanted to see her to let her know that he hadn't been able to get the cream she'd ordered, so he rang the bell. When there was no answer he went round to the back. The door wasn't properly shut, and there were scratches on the woodwork. He still couldn't get any answer, so he called us."

"A professional job?" Craig asked.

Franklin shrugged. "Could have been. It was an old door, and it didn't fit very well. A child could have forced it."

"Where was she?"

"Halfway up the stairs. She'd been hit several times with something like an iron bar. Probably what chummy used to get in."

"Nasty," Craig said. He had liked Ruth Adamson. "Do you know when it happened?"

"According to the doctor, she must have died almost at once, and she'd been dead between five and seven hours when he saw her. That puts it between two-thirty and four-thirty this morning. She was still holding an old-fashioned hairbrush. It looks as if she heard somebody in the house, picked up the only solid thing she had handy, and went to see what it was. The burglar panicked, lashed out at her, and bolted."

"Did he take much?"

"Who knows? She lived on her own, and we haven't been able to trace any close relatives yet; we can't tell what she had. One of the upstairs rooms had been turned over, but he doesn't seem to have tried downstairs, there's some good silver and china there. She must have disturbed him before he'd had time to look round properly, and after he killed her he didn't hang about."

A girl in an apron came from the kitchen with two plates of small, square sandwiches almost concealed by lettuce leaves, rings of raw onion, quartered tomatoes, and slices of cucumber. The sandwiches, of wholemeal bread, were very thin.

"That's a round?" Franklin demanded disgustedly, looking at the plate she handed him. "We'd better have two more, love."

"And I'll have a round of prawn as well as beef," Craig added.

"Prawn's £1.70," Franklin observed grudgingly as the girl departed.

Craig grinned. "I'm on expenses, I'm entitled to a full lunch." He paused. "Could a woman have done it?"

"It's possible, but it doesn't look like a woman's crime. Franklin's tone sharpened. "Have you any reason for asking?"

"No." Craig considered telling Franklin that he had called on Mrs. Adamson yesterday afternoon, but beyond his natural curiosity the inspector had no reason for asking what he was doing in Fawchester. Once he knew that he had seen the dead woman he would have an official reason for asking, and Craig wasn't prepared to tell him. Not yet, at least; later he might have to.

"What are you doing here?" Franklin asked as if he had read the other man's thoughts.

"Just passing through," Craig replied innocently.

The inspector looked unconvinced.

"She used to have a lodger," Salisbury remarked. "A young woman named Thornton. She committed suicide a fortnight ago."

"You think there could be a connection?" Franklin's expression became sceptical. "Why should there be? No, it's just one of those tragic coincidences."

Craig drank some more of his beer, and soon the girl returned with their extra sandwiches. The conversation turned to other topics.

After Franklin and his sergeant had gone Craig sat on in the bar alone. The investigation of Ruth Adamson's murder was nothing to do with him, but he was experienced enough to know that it was bound to make his own job more difficult. People might be reluctant to talk to him with the shadow of a murder hanging over the town, while Franklin wouldn't take kindly to his going round asking questions. Stirring things, he would call it. Putting people on their guard.

Craig was reflecting grimly that he hadn't liked this job from the beginning, and he liked it less all the time, when somebody behind him said, "Hallo, Alan."

He would have known that voice anywhere. It hadn't occurred to him that he might see Leila here, and he looked round quickly. She was wearing yellow trousers and a white cowl-necked sweater under an open white jacket, and at the sight of her he was conscious of an unaccustomed tension inside himself. He stood up.

"You've heard about Ruth?" she asked.

Craig nodded. "Yes. What are you doing here?"

"I wanted to see you." Leila looked round. It was just after one, and the bar was filling up rapidly. "Is there any place quieter we can talk?"

"There's the lounge."

"Let's go there."

"Do you want anything to drink?"

"Not now."

Leila seemed on edge, Craig thought. Naturally she was upset about Ruth Adamson's death, but was there something else?

The lounge, a snug, low ceilinged room with dark panelling and a big open fireplace, was deserted. He waited while Leila seated herself on a rather shabby, comfortable looking settee, and took a fireside chair facing her.

"Some bloody man battered her to death," she said violently. "He ought to be castrated."

"What makes you so sure it was a man?" Craig asked.

She gazed at him, clearly surprised. "It must have been."

"Not necessarily. The police say a woman could have done it."

"They're sexists."

"Some of them. But not in that way.

Don't you think women are capable of murder?"

"Not that sort."

"You're letting your prejudices show," Craig said in a cutting tone. Why did he always react like this to Leila's views? he asked himself. Was it just that her manner, as much almost as what she said, infuriated him, or was there some deeper cause? "How did you hear?"

Leila had flushed with anger, but she answered calmly enough, "Norma rang me. She thought I'd rather hear it from her than see it in the papers or on television."

"You came down from London?" Craig said.

Leila looked surprised. "No, I was at home. I live four miles from here, didn't you know?"

"No."

Leila's anger had subsided and she muttered sadly, "She was such a nice person."

"Yes," Craig agreed. "Why did you want to see me?" Leila didn't answer at once, and he went on. "You spoke to her yesterday evening, didn't you?"

"She called me. How did you know?"

"You knew I was staying here."

"Oh. She said you'd been to see her, and she wondered what you were doing here. It seemed to be worrying her."

"There was no reason why it should, it's nothing to do with her," Craig said. "You still haven't told me what you wanted to see me about."

Again Leila hesitated. "It was something Ruth said in Venice. Alan, there's no question that Mary killed herself, is there?"

"No," Craig answered, eyeing her curiously. "Why?"

"You're sure?"

"Look, she was a neurotic girl, she'd had a row with her boyfriend, there was an empty pill bottle in her waste-paper bin, and we found a suicide note in her writing. People who die by accident don't leave notes."

"I wasn't thinking of accident," Leila said slowly, avoiding Craig's eye.

"Go on."

"We were walking along the Riva, looking at the view and the boats and the sun on the water, and she stopped suddenly and smiled as if she'd just seen something wonderful. I asked her what it was, and she said, "I'm going to kill Francesca." Just like that. "Have you read any of her books?" Craig shook his head. "She has a series character, Francesca Holt. I told her she couldn't. Francesca's so popular, and if she stopped using her, she might lose a lot of readers. She said, 'You don't know how I hate that woman. I loathe and detest her,' and that I didn't have to live with her all the time. There was something in the way she said it, as if she wasn't really thinking about Francesca but a real person.

"Then on the way home on the train she asked me if I ever got the feeling that somebody was following me. I just laughed. But she meant it, about Mary. She said that everywhere she went Mary seemed to be, and that sometimes she — she felt like strangling her."

"We all say that about people at times," Craig objected.

"I know," Leila agreed unhappily. "And I know Ruth didn't kill Mary, she couldn't kill anybody, but it's been on my mind ever since."

"Forget it," Craig advised her. Curious, he asked, "Why did you want to tell me?"

"Because I thought you'd . . ." Leila regarded him angrily. It was as if she resented him, not for himself, but for something in her. "I had to tell somebody, you knew Ruth and you used to be a policeman. I hoped you'd help and tell me what to do."

"You'd better tell the police what you've told me," Craig said. "It's just possible that it may tie in with something they already know."

"It would be like betraying a friend."

"You can't hurt her now. And you were probably the last person to speak to her."

Leila stood up, angry colour in her cheeks. "You're a callous bastard, aren't

224

you?" she accused him bitterly.

"I thought if I told you you couldn't hurt her, it might make it easier," Craig said.

Their eyes met, and it was Leila who looked away first. "Okay," she said in a low voice, "I'll tell them."

"They'll make a note of it, it won't have anything to do with the case, and that'll be the end of it," Craig told her. Then, driven by some devilish impulse, he added, "You don't have to worry about Franklin, he's human. Not like me."

"Why do you always have to put me in the wrong?" Leila demanded.

"Because I'm a sexist." Craig grinned. "You said so."

"And you think it's something to be proud of?"

"No. But I don't believe men and women are the same, either. They're different, with different roles and different capabilities, complementary, not one better than the other. I like little girls to play with dolls and little boys with footballs, you want them to be the same and do the same things."

"I want girls to play football if they want to. For women to be equal."

"As near the same as makes no difference."

"Alan, I . . . " Leila stopped abruptly. "Oh hell, what's the use?" She walked past him to the door. "Thanks for your advice."

The door closed behind her.

Craig knew that he had made a mess of things, but wasn't sure how. He had told Leila to go to the police because he was an ex-copper, and that was the way they thought. It didn't mean that he believed there was the remotest possibility that Ruth Adamson had killed Mary. Nor did Leila, she had come to him for reassurance. And what had he given her?

Nevertheless, two women who lived in the same house had both died violent deaths within a fortnight of each other. Was Franklin right, and it was no more than a tragic coincidence? The note Mary left was written on Hotel Michele paper. Which must mean that she had made up her mind to kill herself by Saturday morning at the latest, because even if she had taken some paper from the hotel with her, surely at the end she wouldn't have looked for it when there was a supply of stationery handy on the table beside her orange juice?

When Craig walked through the lounge after Ruth Adamson's talk Mary was there writing a letter. At least, he had assumed it to be a letter. She seemed to be having difficulty finding the words she wanted, but she hadn't looked distressed. Nor had she done earlier at dinner, she had been chatting animatedly about her book. Even more significantly, surely no one with her temperament who intended to commit suicide within a few hours could have behaved as normally on the train as she had done?

Everything hinged on the letter she had left. Craig believed he knew the explanation of that, but if he was right, Mary Thornton hadn't killed herself. She had been murdered too, and that would open up a whole new picture.

Ruth Adamson's cabin had been next to Mary's, could she have seen or heard something that night, something which made her a danger to Mary's murderer, and that was why she was killed? If so, Craig thought, she hadn't appreciated the significance of what she knew, he was pretty sure that her shock the next morning when he told her what had happened was genuine. And if she suspected that Mary had been murdered, she would have gone to the police, either in France or as soon as she got home.

He frowned. Something was bothering him, something he had seen in Mary's cabin. What was it?

He must talk to Norma Paget.

10

THE clouds had blown away and the sun was shining from a clear blue sky as Craig turned left out of the hotel and set off down the hill. Across the street the little crowd of spectators had dispersed, satisfied that there was more for them to see.

Norma's assistants were still at lunch, and when Craig walked in she was alone behind the counter; dealing with two girls asking about winter holidays in Tenerife. While he waited Craig studied the racks of brochures. One of these days, he told himself, he would go somewhere really exotic like Nepal or Tahiti. "When my ship comes in," his grandmother used to say. People didn't say that any longer, they said, "When I win the pools." Somehow it wasn't the same. Not that there was much chance of his ship coming in until he was too old to care, he thought wryly.

Unbidden, the idea of Leila's going with him came into his mind, and he realised that he was thinking of her in a way he hadn't thought of any woman since Jean died. It was daft they couldn't speak to each other without arguing. He wasn't even sure he liked her very much. Indeed, there were times when he actively disliked her. She was most of the things he hated and resented in a woman, and she had made it plain that she couldn't stand his sort of man. The pity of it was that when she dropped her militant feminist pose she was completely different.

The girls departed and Norma looked round and saw him. "Alan!" she exclaimed. "What are you doing here?" A flicker of concern shadowed her plump, pretty features. "You got our cheque all right, didn't you? I know Mike posted it."

"Yes, thanks very much," Craig assured her.

"You've heard about Ruth?"

"Yes."

"It's awful, isn't it? They say she disturbed a burglar. A thing like that happening here!"

Presumably even Fawchester was subject to the normal human passions, Craig thought. Greed, fear, jealousy. Subject to crime too.

"What brings you here?" Norma enquired.

"A job. Nothing to do with Ruth. I was passing and I suddenly thought of something. You must have had the puzzle I was supposed to solve on the train all worked out, hadn't you?"

"Yes. The murder was going to happen in our cabin. Mike's and mine. What about it?"

"Who was to be the victim?"

"Betty Layton."

Craig saw his half formed theory collapsing. He had seen Betty's handwriting, she had insisted on writing out a card for everybody to sign at dinner on the Orient Express, and it was neat and round, nothing like Mary Thornton's

231

rather spiky hand. "Did she know?" he asked.

"Yes, of course. I told her after Ruth's talk." With a touch of malice Norma added, "If you want to know, I rather enjoyed telling her."

It didn't fit, Craig thought. He must be on the wrong track. Then he saw that it didn't necessarily matter who was to be the 'victim' in the game. "What about the murderer?" he enquired. "Who was that to be?"

"Mary. She was supposed to have shot Betty and left a suicide note beside the body." Norma stared at Craig. "What is all this, Alan? You can't think — "

"Half a minute," Craig said. "You told Mary that evening too, didn't you? And you asked her to write the note. It had to be in her writing for my benefit when I started asking questions." Norma nodded. "Did she show it to you after she'd written it?"

"Yes. She was rather pleased with it."

"What did it say?" Craig asked, tense. Everything depended on Norma's answer.

"Something about 'It's too much to bear. After what you did I can't go on. This is the only way I'll ever get any peace now'. I can't remember exactly."

Norma remembered very well, Craig thought.

"Oh my God!" she said. She looked horrified. "That's terrible. It's as if she was really writing about herself."

"Yes," Craig agreed grimly. He had been right, the letter he found in Mary's pocket wasn't a genuine suicide note, it was the one she had written the previous evening for Norma's game. Had someone else known about it and used it? "Did Michael see the note?" he asked.

A wary look came into Norma's eye, but she answered readily enough. "I don't think so. He'd gone out before she finished it, and she can't have shown it to him after he got back because Ruth had taken her up to bed by then."

"What about the next day?"

"I'm sure she didn't."

Which explained why Paget hadn't said anything about its having been written for the game when it turned up in Mary's pocket after her death, Craig reflected. He didn't know. Or did he, and he had kept quiet for his own reasons? For that matter, Norma might be lying now to protect him.

"What difference does it make?" she asked bitterly. "I wish I'd never thought of the bloody trip. It was so lovely in Venice, yet everything seemed to go wrong somehow, and half the people were sniping at each other all the time. Most of the rest were on edge. Even Paula Renton, and she's usually so calm."

"Why should she be on edge?" Craig enquired innocently. Norma looked as if she were going to say something, then changed her mind. "I've no idea," she answered.

"What about Mary Thornton?" Craig asked. "I must say she didn't seem depressed to me. I had dinner at the same table as her that evening in Venice, and she was talking about the book she was going to write. She seemed happy enough."

"I don't know," Norma said flatly.

"What did you make of her?"

"I didn't think much about her." There was a hint of defiance in Norma's tone, and in the way she looked at Craig. "To be honest, I didn't care for her. I suppose I shouldn't say it now, but she was sly and I . . . " She stopped abruptly, the colour flooding her cheeks under her make-up. But it was a flush of anger not embarrassment, Craig thought. He waited, and after a few seconds she went on as if she couldn't stop herself, "I can't think what men saw in her."

Craig was surprised. Personally he hadn't thought Mary was attractive, either in her looks or her personality, but that didn't mean that other men hadn't. Or one man. Had Paget cast his eye in that direction and not been repulsed? If so, it might have caused the row he had heard in the Pagets' cabin on the Orient Express.

"What is all this about?" Norma demanded. "She's dead, and I'm sorry she killed herself. But it's over and done with now."

"I'm not so sure," Craig told her. "It's possible she didn't commit suicide."

There was no mistaking the fear in Norma's eyes now. "You mean . . . ?" she faltered.

"She may have been murdered," Craig said brutally.

Norma's carefully made-up features seemed to fall apart. Suddenly she looked much older. "Oh God!" she breathed.

"You knew, didn't you?"

"No. No."

One of the assistants came through from the back of the building, letting the door slam behind her. Norma seemed unable to take her eyes off Craig's face. The girl glanced curiously at her, sat down behind the counter and began dictating a letter.

Her noisy entrance was an intrusion. Craig sensed that Norma was relieved by it, yet at the same time angered by the girl's lack of understanding. He walked out, leaving Norma staring after him.

When he got back to the Golden Hart Sue told him that there was a call for him. Running up the stairs, he closed his door and picked up the phone.

It was Dave Smith. "Are you alone?" he asked.

"I'm not sure," Craig answered. It was unlikely that Sue was listening, but he had learnt to be careful.

Smith understood. "All right. We've made some enquiries where you said. Your people are staying there, but not husband and wife; he's using his real name, and she's registered as Mrs. Pamela Brown, without an 'e.' They both have rooms on the third floor, close but not adjoining, and, according to the staff, they spend a lot of time together. The impression is that they're having it off, but being fairly discreet about it. She seems nervous, they say. That's about all."

"Thanks very much."

"Do you want me to take it any farther?"

"Not at this stage." Craig said goodbye

and replaced the phone.

So Paula Renton had lied when she told Ruth Adamson she was going to Yorkshire, she was staying at the same Kensington hotel as Clive Winters, and seeing a lot of him there. It was the old, old story.

There was a knock on the door, too peremptory for any of the staff, and Craig swore under his breath. It was his own fault, he had known that Franklin's men would question all Mrs. Adamson's neighbours and that the owner of the bookshop was bound to tell them he had called on Ruth yesterday afternoon. Moreover he hadn't expected the inspector to be pleased when he knew.

He was right. Franklin was angry, and it suited him for Craig to see he was. He strode in without being invited, Salisbury behind him. The sergeant shut the door and remained standing with his back to it.

"You withheld information," Franklin said accusingly. When he was angry his facial muscles tightened, making him look leaner than ever.

"What information?" Craig asked him.

"You know bloody well what information. You knew Ruth Adamson and you went to see her yesterday afternoon. So far, you're the last person to have seen her alive."

"Except whoever killed her."

Franklin eyed Craig as if he hadn't been excluding the murderer. "What did you go to see her about?" he demanded.

"I hoped she might be able to tell me something."

"What?"

Craig suppressed a flippant rejoinder. Franklin wouldn't have appreciated it. "Nothing that's relevant to your enquiries," he said.

"I'll decide what's relevant."

"It was information about a job I'm doing. She couldn't tell me anything, so it can't be relevant." Craig knew that that didn't necessarily follow, but he believed it to be true in this case and he hoped that Franklin would accept it.

The inspector gave him a bleak look.

"What is this job you're on?"

Craig shook his head. "You can take my word it's nothing to do with Mrs. Adamson."

"So why did you go to see her?"

"I told you, I hoped she might be able to help, but I was wrong."

Franklin's eyes hadn't left Craig's face, now he asked, "How well did you know her?"

"Hardly at all. The travel agents here, Pagets, ran a trip to Venice the week before last. Fly out, four days there, and come back on the Orient Express. She went to give a talk on Agatha Christie, and I joined them on the last day. They hired me to solve some sort of murder game on the train coming home, but it was cancelled when Mary Thornton died."

"She committed suicide."

"So they said."

There was a brief, tense silence.

"Are you saying she didn't?" Franklin demanded.

"Look, the suicide note was a fake, it

240

was one she'd written for the game. And if you were going to kill yourself and you'd written a letter explaining why, you wouldn't tuck it away in a jacket pocket, you'd leave it somewhere where it would be found straightaway. That's two things. Third, that evening, right up to an hour or two before she's supposed to have taken the pills, she was perfectly normal. I saw her in the bar laughing and talking. Fourth, on the Friday evening in Venice she came back to the hotel soaked to the skin and swearing that somebody had pushed her into the canal as she was getting off a water bus. Have you ever been on one of those buses?" Franklin shook his head. "They're like small ferries. It'd be impossible to fall in if you were just jostled by accident, there are rails round the sides, and they pull right in to the stops before the gate in the rail's opened. Either she jumped, or somebody pushed her, deliberately and hard."

Again there was a tense pause. Through the open window Craig could hear the traffic in the High Street. It seemed curiously remote.

"If she wanted to commit suicide," he went on, "she had the pills handy. Why try to drown herself in that filthy water and risk being crushed and maybe not killed?"

The other men regarded him steadily. Their expressions gave nothing away.

"Why should anybody want to kill her?" Franklin demanded.

Craig shrugged. "Why should anybody want to kill anybody? She wasn't everyone's top of the pops. She'd had a row with one of her boy-friends earlier that day, and I have an idea that she and Paget had something going and his wife found out about it. Just about the time she must have gone in the water I was walking back to the hotel with one of the others, and we heard a commotion at the bus stop. A splash and a lot of shouting. A minute or so later Paget passed us coming from that direction, and Grundy, the boy-friend, followed us into the hotel just afterwards."

"You're suggesting one of them tried to kill her then, and when they didn't they made sure on the train?" Franklin's tone was scathing.

"I'm not suggesting anything. Except that somebody killed her. Either of them could have pushed her in the canal. So could Paget's wife, she wasn't in the lounge or the bar when we got back to the hotel. Nor were most of the rest of the party, come to that."

"All right," Franklin conceded grudgingly, "maybe she was murdered. What's the connection with our case here?"

"Don't ask me," Craig told him. "But it's more than one of your tragic coincidences if there isn't one."

"You're still not going to tell me why you went to see Mrs. Adamson yesterday?"

"Not yet."

Franklin glared. "If I find you're obstructing our enquiries . . . " he said threateningly.

By the door Salisbury stirred as if to reinforce the warning. Craig told himself that Franklin was making a gesture. It was something that he felt he owed himself. And perhaps Salisbury. The situation had changed in the last two or three minutes, and he was no longer on the defensive; he had given Franklin too much to think about. But he knew that that state of affairs might not last long.

"We'll get on to the French police and see if they can tell us anything," Franklin said, his manner implying that he was making a concession.

"If I were you, I'd get hold of a list of the people who went to Venice and see how many of them could have killed Mrs. Adamson," Craig told him.

The inspector walked to the door. "Don't push your luck too far, Craig," he warned. There was a steely, unforgiving note in his voice.

Salisbury gave Craig a long, searching look, and followed Franklin out of the room.

They had left the door open behind them. Craig satisfied himself that they had really gone, and closed it before he picked up the phone and dialled Colonel Renton's number. As before the colonel answered himself.

"Craig," Craig told him. "I need to see you."

"Have you discovered anything?" Renton asked anxiously.

"I'll tell you when I see you," Craig said. "I've just had a visit from the inspector in charge of the Ruth Adamson enquiries. He wanted to know why I'm here and who I'm working for. I haven't told him yet, but I'll probably have to."

"No!" Renton said forcefully. "All right, you'd better come here."

"Six o'clock?" Craig suggested.

"Very well."

"Have you got the statements I asked you for?"

"Yes." Bitterly the colonel added, "I wish to God I'd never started this."

He was going to regret it even more soon, Craig thought. He was sorry for Renton.

After he put the phone down he sat

for several seconds gazing at it. He had just remembered what it was he had seen in Mary Thornton's cabin that had bothered him: the empty pill bottle in the waste-paper bin. Two things about that little bottle seemed to contradict each other. First, the cap was on, and Craig doubted whether even the tidiest suicide would trouble to replace the cap before dropping a bottle into a bin. It was one more indication that Mary hadn't killed herself. But there had been two soiled paper tissues half covering the bottle. Almost certainly Mary had put them there herself; surely she must have seen the bottle and wondered what it was doing there?

Perhaps she had. It was a trivial point, anyway, but the murderer, if there was one, had been so careful in everything else. That bottle didn't fit, it was the only piece of hard evidence which pointed to Mary's having committed suicide. Unless the murderer had dropped it into the bin after she was dead to bolster the case for her having killed herself, and deliberately half concealed it under the tissues. If so, it must have been done either during the night, or that morning before the doctor was called. And the only member of the party who had been in the cabin then was Paget.

Peter Grundy lived with his mother in a conventional fifty-year-old semi-detached house on the edge of the town. The house had red brick walls, a mock-Tudor gable, and bow windows upstairs and down intended to signify its superiority over the bay windows (downstairs only) and stone-dash of the houses farther up the road. At five minutes past three Craig walked up the short path to the front door and rang the bell. As he had hoped, Grundy was at school and his mother at home. He explained that he had met Peter in Venice and added, untruthfully, that he had hoped he might find him in.

"It's nothing important," he said. "Just something I wanted to ask him about the trip. I didn't mean to trouble you."

"You've no call to be apologising," Mrs. Grundy assured him. "I don't get that many visitors nowadays I'm sorry to see another. Come in."

Although she had lived for over forty years in the South of England, Muriel Grundy clung resolutely to the Yorkshire accent of her childhood and prided herself on her bluntness. She was a big-boned woman with grey hair, large features, and rather protuberant eyes. Craig wasn't sure whether the lines round her mouth were a symptom of disillusionment or pain, she was stooped with rheumatism.

He followed her into a sitting room with the curiously dated appearance and atmosphere of a best parlour used only on Sundays and special occasions. There was an over-tidy formality, a stiffness about it which made him feel slightly ill at ease. Through the open door of the dining room across the hall he glimpsed a half-empty bottle of sweet sherry, a glass on the table beside it, and wondered if that was why Mrs. Grundy had chosen to bring him in here. He could smell the wine on her breath, but she appeared to be quite sober.

"Sit you down," she told him a little too effusively. "I'll just go and put the kettle on. You'd like a cup of tea, wouldn't you?"

Craig sat down, but declined the tea, and the old woman — she must be well over seventy, he reckoned — sat opposite him, watchful, waiting to hear what he had wanted to see her son about. She had been telling the truth when she said that few people came to see her now. She had never settled comfortably into the town, which was too different from Barnsley where she had been born and grown up, but that hadn't mattered very much while her husband was alive. If she knew that people accepted her for his sake she bore the knowledge with her customary blend of stoicism and indifference, and devoted herself to caring for Peter. Now her husband was dead, and it made it no easier that she understood that the cause of her isolation was in herself. Widowed, with a son she didn't understand, and for whom sometimes she feared, she was lonely, and too proud to admit her loneliness. She knew very little about what had happened in Venice and on the Orient Express beyond the bare facts of Mary's suicide. Peter had told her practically nothing, and his reluctance to talk made her afraid for him. He had never been in love before, and he had taken Mary's death badly.

"I had to come to Fawchester on a job," Craig explained. "You've heard about Mrs. Adamson?"

"Ay. It's a terrible thing to happen."

"I know the inspector who's in charge, and I ran into him at lunchtime. I gather they think now that Mary Thornton was murdered too," Craig said. They should by now, anyway, he thought. Even if they hadn't before.

Muriel's expression revealed nothing of the fear she felt. "What makes them think that?" she asked.

"Something they've been told I expect. What was she like?"

"Sly. That's what I thought. A real trouble-maker."

"Other people said that," Craig observed. He hoped that if Mrs. Grundy knew she wasn't the only one to harbour such thoughts about Mary, she might be encouraged to tell him more.

But she wasn't so easily persuaded. "Why are you interested in her?" she demanded suspiciously. "You didn't know her, did you?"

"Not very well," Craig admitted. "But I was on the train, and I knew Mrs. Adamson. From what the inspector said, it looks as if they think whoever killed her killed Mary too. What did you think of her, part from her being sly?"

"I didn't like her, I make no bones about that. But she's dead now, and it makes no road what I thought while she was alive," Muriel said. "Or what Peter did either, if that's what you're thinking."

"Peter?" Craig said. "But he liked her, didn't he? I mean, I thought . . ."

He stopped invitingly, but the old

woman didn't respond. She was more on the defensive than she wanted him to see, he thought. Her worn, twisted hands were gripping the arms of her chair so tightly that he could see the blotches standing out on her skin, and for the first time he saw her as lonely and afraid rather than awkward and blunt to the point of rudeness. Was her fear for herself or her son? he wondered. Did she suspect that Peter had killed first Mary Thornton, then Ruth Adamson?

"What did they quarrel about in Venice?" he asked quietly.

"Who says they quarrelled?"

"Everyone knows they did."

"Everyone knows a sight too much," Muriel observed grimly.

"Or not enough," Craig suggested. "If you know just part of something, you don't know the truth about it."

She eyed him appraisingly. "Are you thinking of anything in particular?"

"No."

"Playing up to Peter like she did. Leading him on, then telling him there was somebody else."

"Do you know who it was?"

"It was obvious, it was that Clive Winters. Peter said she was all over him the last evening in Venice and on the train. She couldn't leave him alone."

She was exaggerating, Craig thought. Or her son had exaggerated to her. And his argument with Mary had occurred before then. Remembering the girl's forlorn expression when Grundy stormed out of the bar that lunchtime and the way she had looked at him later, he suspected that she had turned to Winters only because he had shown interest in her book, and the 'somebody else' had been Paget.

Craig wondered what there had been between them. Less, perhaps, than Mary had wanted to believe, at least on Paget's side, whatever Norma thought. Had Paget wanted to end it? Or perhaps Mary, seeing no future in their relationship, had turned to Grundy. Craig would have put her down as lonely almost to the point of desperation rather than promiscuous. But then, he reminded himself, he had seen very little of her.

"You didn't come here to talk about her," Muriel said bluntly. "Why did you?"

"I told you, there was something I wanted to ask Peter about," Craig answered. Like many old people, she was a strange mixture of shrewdness and self-deception, he thought. It was the prerogative of the old to close their eyes to a good deal that they didn't want to see. Her tragedy was that she was finding now that there were things she couldn't close them to.

"There was a Mrs. Renton out there," he remarked.

"I know. Peter told me."

"I gathered that she's a big noise round here."

"You could say so," Muriel acknowledged grudgingly. "The Rentons are all right, I dare say. I don't have anything to do with people like them."

So she couldn't tell him anything about Mrs. Renton, Craig told himself.

He hadn't expected she would. Nor Grundy. He gave the impression of being so absorbed in his own troubles that he hardly noticed anybody else.

"Peter'll be in this evening, I expect," Muriel said.

"I might come back later then," Craig told her.

She nodded, and he didn't know whether she believed anything he had told her or not.

As soon as he could he left.

11

FAWCHESTER COURT stood high on a shelf of the Downs. At one minute past six Craig turned off the main road on to a drive which ran for a quarter of a mile through a wood of oaks, beeches, and birches before emerging into a wide open space. The house stood in the centre of the space, a handsome building of pale, mellow red brick with three rows of rectangular windows and a modest portico. More cloud had blown up during the last hour, and a cool little breeze stirred the tops of the trees.

Craig parked his Triumph in front of the house, got out and tugged the wrought iron bell pull. The resultant clang somewhere deep inside the house was answered by Renton himself so quickly that Craig wondered if he had been waiting near the door for him to ring. Was Renton nervous, or merely eager?

"We'll talk on the lawn," the colonel said brusquely.

Craig glanced up at the sky and reckoned that, if they talked fast, they might finish before the rain started.

They walked in silence round the side of the house, across the corner of a wide terrace and down four steps on to a broad expanse of lawn bordered on three sides by rose beds. At least, Craig told himself, they wouldn't be overheard, there was nothing but air and closely mown grass for a good forty yards in any direction.

"Why did you want to see me?" Renton demanded.

"Have you got the statements?"

"Yes." With evident distaste the colonel took an envelope from his pocket and handed it to Craig. "I don't like this," he complained bitterly.

"You needn't feel too badly," Craig told him. The flap of the envelope was stuck down. He ripped it open, extracted four sheets of computer printed bank

257

statements and scanned them quickly. What he had half expected to see was there, and he gave them back.

"Well?" Renton demanded.

"You hired me to try to find out why Mrs. Renton was worried," Craig said. "You made out you'd no idea what the trouble was, but you thought she was being blackmailed, didn't you?"

For a moment the colonel didn't speak, then he said as if Craig were forcing the admission from him, "I was afraid it might be that."

"I warned you that there might be another man, Colonel."

"Are you saying there is?"

Almost gently Craig answered, "He went on the Pagets' trip to Venice and for the past three days he and Mrs. Renton have been staying at the Crosslands Hotel in Kensington. They didn't book in as man and wife, but they have rooms close to each other on the same floor, and they've spent a lot of time together. She's registered as Mrs. Pamela Brown."

Renton stopped and stared at his companion. "That isn't my wife," he exclaimed. "Mrs. Renton came home half an hour ago. That's why I brought you out here. You've got hold of the wrong woman."

"She was there last night," Craig told him. "I'm sorry, Colonel."

Like a man clinging to a hope he knows is forlorn, Renton said, "You say they weren't registered as man and wife, and they didn't share a room."

"That doesn't necessarily mean anything, except that they were being careful."

"I don't believe it."

Craig had been sorry for the colonel, he was an old man and his wife was a faithless, supercilious bitch, whatever people like Ruth Adamson said about her, but he was losing patience with him now. Renton had used him.

"You've known all along, haven't you?" he demanded angrily. "You didn't hire me to find out what was worrying her, you wanted somebody you could blame in your own mind for destroying your illusions."

Suddenly the colonel looked ten years older. The lines on his face had deepened and the flesh had sagged. "No," he said quietly, with a touching dignity, "I didn't know. But I'm not a fool, I realised it was possible. Who is he?"

"His name's Winters. He's the sales manager at the brewery here."

"My God!"

It was impossible to tell whether the bitter exclamation was a sign of the old man's despair, or disgust that his wife had taken a salesman for a lover. Craig hoped it was the first.

"At this stage there isn't any firm evidence of misconduct," he said, his tone deliberately business-like and impersonal. "I expect I can get it if you want me to, but your instructions were just to find out what was worrying her."

For almost a minute Renton said nothing. They walked on slowly, their shoes making foot prints in the grass, still wet from the rain earlier.

"No," he said at last with the air of a man who, after a moment's weakness, has regained control of both himself and of the situation. "I suppose you'll send me a report. Let me have your account with it, and I'll send you a cheque." Turning, he began to walk towards the house.

"There's something else," Craig told him. "Your wife's bank is about the only one whose statements still show the payees of cheques. She's drawn one to 'Cash' for £250 at the beginning of every month for the last four months. Does she use that account for settling your household bills?"

"No," Renton replied. "We have a joint house account."

"Anyway, she'd hardly pay them in cash."

The colonel stopped to face the younger man. "Go on," he said.

"I think she's giving Winters money, and making the cheques out to 'Cash' so that his name doesn't appear on her statements."

Two angry spots of colour showed in the colonel's cheeks. "What are you suggesting?" he demanded harshly.

"That she's either giving him regular presents — or he's blackmailing her," Craig replied.

The two men stood staring at each other. Then the colonel said roughly, "You've done what I hired you to do, now you can forget it."

"It isn't as easy as that," Craig told him. "If he is blackmailing her, that's a crime. And if you cover it up, apart from anything else, you're guilty of aiding and abetting it."

"I'll worry about that."

"All right. But the police are pushing me. They want to know why I went to see Mrs. Adamson yesterday afternoon."

"It had nothing to do with Mrs. Renton or me."

Craig eyed the older man. "You're wrong, Colonel," he said. "I went to see her because she knew your wife better than anyone else I knew. She might have known what was worrying her."

"I told you — " Renton began angrily.

"You needn't worry, I was very discreet." But not discreet enough to fool Ruth Adamson, Craig thought. "I don't like withholding information from the police, and they don't like me doing it. I shall have to tell them."

"No!"

"Look, I'm the one they'll do for obstructing them. It's my job, I'm not prepared to stick my neck out that far. Not for you, Colonel."

Again there was a silence before Renton said grudgingly, "Very well. But only if it's absolutely necessary. And I don't want Mrs. Renton brought into it."

He was still concerned for her, Craig thought. Even now. He couldn't make up his mind whether the old man's attitude was admirable or stupid.

"I may not be able to avoid it," he said brutally. "You don't seem to understand, Colonel. Mary Thornton didn't commit suicide, she was murdered. There were seven people in that coach on the Orient Express knew her, and now one of them has been killed. Your wife was one of the others. There's no way anyone can mess about with a murder enquiry. Not even you."

He expected Renton to react angrily, but the colonel said only with a quiet dignity, "Do you think I would try to?"

"I don't know," Craig told him. "It might depend on who you thought the murderer was."

They faced each other. Overhead the clouds were massing angrily and it was half dark on the lawn. Someone had switched on a light in one of the ground floor windows of the house but out here it only emphasised the gloom. The colonel was fighting to control his anger, but behind it Craig believed he could see something else. Fear.

"I'll send you my report," he said.

Turning, he walked away across the grass, leaving the colonel alone in the middle of the big lawn.

As he reached the corner of the terrace a french door at the back of the house opened and a woman stepped out. It was Paula Renton. For a second or two she stared at him, then she turned and started walking towards her husband. Craig went on to his car.

Paula had recognised him at once, and she had no illusions about his reason for being there. She had dreaded this moment for months. Now it had come, and she gathered her courage and resolution round her like a cloak as she crossed the lawn, her heels sinking into the soft turf and the breeze cold on her cheeks.

Renton waited for her. He said nothing, nor did he move.

"That was that man Craig." The muscles in Paula's throat felt tight, and she was surprised how normal the words sounded. "What did he come here for?"

"I hired him," Renton told her.

"Why?"

"You'd seemed so worried lately, and you wouldn't tell me what was wrong."

"So you went to him?" Paula asked bitterly.

"Yes. I wish to God I hadn't."

"What did he tell you?"

"Don't you know?" The colonel made himself meet his wife's gaze. "That you didn't go to Yorkshire, you've been staying at a hotel in Kensington, and a man who was in Venice with you was there too. You spent a lot of time together."

"Oh God!" Paula breathed.

"You've been giving him money, haven't you?"

"Did Craig find that out too?"

"I had to show him your bank statements." The colonel avoided his wife's eye. "That man's blackmailing you, isn't he, Paula?"

Paula shook her head. She cared so desperately, she thought. Yet now she felt she hardly cared at all any more. It was as if she had been physically beaten.

"What are you going to do?" she asked.

"Do?" It seemed that the colonel hadn't considered that. "I don't know.

I wish I'd never thought of going to Craig."

"Then why did you?" Paula asked him in a tortured voice.

"Because I was worried about you."

"Oh, you fool!" There was love and understanding as well as desperation in the cry. "You don't see what you've done."

They gazed at each other, fear and helplessness in both their faces.

Craig parked in his usual place in the yard behind the Golden Hart and walked back to the street. As he was turning to enter the hotel a woman behind him exclaimed, "Alan! Fancy seeing you!"

There was no mistaking that voice, and Craig turned reluctantly. "Hallo, Betty," he said. Betty Layton was the last person he would have wanted to encounter while he was here, by tomorrow it would be all over the town that he was in Fawchester, with heaven only knew what embellishments.

"What are you doing in Fawchester?"

she enquired brightly. "Oh, I suppose it's something to do with that awful business about Ruth."

"That's nothing to do with me," Craig told her firmly. "I was just passing through, and I thought I'd stop for something to eat. This place looked okay." He couldn't care less if she found out later he was lying, he thought. You had to lie to people like Betty, the truth was too dangerous a commodity to be entrusted to them, and by the time she knew he would have gone.

Betty looked arch. "You don't really expect me to believe that, do you?"

"I chase debts and look for people who've gone missing, not murderers."

"I think you're helping the police."

Craig forced a laugh. "They wouldn't want my help." He was wearing only a lightweight jacket, while Betty was wrapped up in a mack and carrying an umbrella. Any minute now it would start to rain, probably hard, and he would have an excuse for escaping.

"Ruth was nice," Betty remarked

ingenuously. "She was never catty like some people."

For self-deception that took some beating, Craig thought. Amazingly, she sounded as if she meant it.

"No," he agreed.

"It always surprised me her sharing her house with Mary. They were so different."

"In what way?"

"Well, Ruth was quiet and sensible, and Mary was all up or all down. And she was out for all she could get. Especially men. Well, you know." Betty grimaced archly. "Norma couldn't stand her because she tried to score with Mike. Not that she got very far there, if you ask me. And she was inquisitive, too, always poking around asking questions."

"She was writing a book."

"Oh, don't we all know! She was always talking about it. You'd have thought she was Emily Bronte or Catherine Cookson or somebody. And the way she went round trying to dig up things about people here." Betty giggled. "I wonder if she ever found out anything she shouldn't have."

"What sort of thing?" Craig enquired. He wasn't interested in Betty's gossip, but some comment seemed to be required, if only to get rid of her as quickly as possible.

"Oh, anything," Betty answered vaguely. Clearly she had spoken without thinking what she really meant. If she had meant anything. "I must dash, we've a rehearsal this evening: the Fawchester Players. We're doing *Present Laughter*. It's by Noel Coward, and it's really ever so good. I'm the girl who wants to sleep with the great star." She giggled again. "Honestly! He's about seventy and a real old woman. Oh well! 'Bye, Alan. It's been lovely seeing you again."

"'Bye," Craig said. Thank Christ, he thought.

As Betty hurried off down the street thunder rumbled menacingly in the distance and the rain started. Craig pushed through the hotel's swing doors, reflecting that if Betty ever murdered anyone, by the time the body was discovered she would have told half the population of Fawchester.

He bought an evening paper from Sue and took it into the bar. The plump barmaid was talking to three men. She drew Craig's beer, put his money in the till, and went to resume the conversation he had interrupted. Craig opened his *Standard.* There was a report of the murder on page two, but it told him nothing that he didn't already know, and he turned to the sports pages. Arsenal were at home to Spurs this evening; if he hadn't been stuck here, he would have been on his way to Highbury by now.

He turned the page again. But now he hardly saw what he was reading, something Betty Layton had said was going round and round in his brain. She had been prattling on about Mary Thornton, her remarks spiced with her usual mix of malice and innuendo, when she said, giggling, "I wonder if she ever found out anything she shouldn't have."

Ever since he became convinced that

Mary had been murdered Craig had assumed that her killer was driven by jealousy or fear of her revealing their relationship, now he saw another possibility. Could Mary have learnt something in the course of her researches? Something which was so dangerous to one of the other members of the Pagets' party that he — or she? — had killed her to preserve their secret?

All the evidence seemed to point to Ruth Adamson's murderer being a burglar she had disturbed while he was robbing her house. But did it? The killer had struck her repeatedly, that suggested that he had meant to kill her. An ordinary burglar might have lashed out once, even twice, but more likely he would simply have pushed her out of his way and bolted. True, this one might be a psychopath, but Craig thought it unlikely.

There were other things. Ruth's body had been found halfway up the stairs; it looked as if the murderer had finished looking upstairs when she came on him.

Yet, according to Franklin, only one room had been disturbed.

The more he thought about it, the more Craig became convinced that it was Mary Thornton's death which was the key to all that had happened, not Ruth Adamson's. The girl wasn't popular — both Mrs. Adamson and Norma Paget had called her sly, while Betty Layton, more or less echoing Mrs. Grundy, had suggested that she chased men — but who had hated or feared her enough to try to drown her, and when that failed, to poison her? Her death hadn't resulted from a moment's passion, it had been carefully and cold-bloodedly planned.

Despite Leila Davidson's anxieties, even if Ruth hadn't been killed herself, Craig couldn't believe that she would have been a serious suspect. From what he had seen of her, she was no chatterer, and she would have kept her feelings about Mary to herself if she had been planning to kill her.

He glanced at his watch; it was eight

minutes to seven. Libraries often closed at seven. Downing the rest of his beer, he hurried out of the hotel and across the street.

The ground floor of the old house had been gutted and converted into a lobby area and two rooms which housed the lending and children's libraries; the reference and record libraries and the offices were on the upper floors. Craig asked the girl at the enquiries desk if he could see the head librarian.

"I'll see if she's free," the girl said.

She went out through a side door, to reappear after two or three minutes with a youngish auburn-haired woman in a jumper and skirt.

"I'm Jane Baldwin, the head librarian," the latter said. "Can I help you?"

"I do a bit of writing, and I'm thinking about doing a history of Fawchester," Craig explained. "Only somebody's told me that one of your staff's writing one already. I wouldn't have bothered you, but I'm afraid I don't know their name."

"You mean Mary Thornton." Miss Baldwin's pleasant face clouded. "She was my deputy. She was planning one, she'd done quite a lot of the preliminary work for it. She died a fortnight ago."

"Oh," Craig said. "I'm sorry."

"Yes, it was a terrible shock to all of us." More briskly the librarian went on, "So there won't be another book, as far as I know."

"Do you happen to know how far she'd got?" Craig enquired. "I mean, if she'd been to see a lot of people, I wouldn't want to bother them again too soon."

"I don't I'm afraid. She'd spent quite a lot of time at the *Chronicle* offices, reading through old issues, that I do know. She showed me her notebooks once, full of notes she'd made, but I don't know any more." Jane Baldwin paused. "It's time there was a new history of Fawchester. The last one was written over eighty years ago and so many people have moved here I'm sure there'd be a lot of interest in it."

"I'll see what I can do," Craig promised.

"Thank you for your help; I'm sorry I was so late."

"That's all right." Miss Baldwin smiled. "I should think her notebooks are still with her other things in her flat; perhaps her family might be prepared to come to some arrangement to let you use them."

Craig stared at her. Why hadn't he thought of the notebooks before? Mary herself had said that evening in Venice that she had left them behind.

"Yes," he agreed. "Yes, they would help a lot."

"Well, let us know if there's anything else we can do," Miss Baldwin told him brightly. "We have quite a good local interest section here."

Craig thanked her again, and started to leave. At the door he asked, "What was that cobbled bit outside the Golden Hart used for?"

The librarian smiled. "That was where the gallows used to stand," she said.

Craig walked back to the hotel. He mustn't let himself be carried away by his new idea, his original theory, that Mary

276

Thornton had been murdered because of her relationship with either Paget or Grundy, still seemed the most likely one. After all, she had been researching the Fawchester of two centuries and more ago, what could she have discovered that could possibly constitute a threat to anyone alive now?

On the other hand, Norma had made no secret of her dislike of the girl. Assuming that Paget had been having it off with Mary, how long had his wife known? If she had found out only since Mary's death, he might have killed her to prevent Norma learning. Unsuccessfully, as it turned out. If it was longer, Norma herself would have had a motive. And their argument on the Orient Express had occurred before Mary died.

Not that the Pagets were the only people who might have wished her dead. According to old Mrs. Grundy, her son and Mary had quarrelled because the girl had told him that there was another man in her life, and Grundy was a morose sod who might well turn violent.

It was just about conceivable that either Paula Renton or Winters might have killed Mary to stop her telling the colonel about their affair, but they must have known that other people were aware of it, so what would have been the point? And of the others, it was hard to see what motive Betty Layton or Leila could have had.

None of the motives seemed very strong on the face of it, but Craig knew only too well that the reasons for murder often appeared tragically inadequate to everyone except the murderer.

For what seemed to him sound reasons Ruth Adamson had been convinced that Mary's story was true and she had been pushed into the canal. It was reasonable to assume that whoever pushed her was the murderer, so who had had the opportunity to both push her as she stepped off the *vaporetto* and, later, to poison her? Ruth Adamson had been in the lounge at the Michele when Mary was pushed, and Betty Layton was in the bar. Leila had been with him. She had been sure that it was Paget who passed them coming from the direction of the San Zaccaria bus stop, and, besides Grundy, who had entered the hotel from the Riva a few minutes later, Mrs. Renton, Winters, and Norma Paget were all unaccounted for.

Five people, then, had had both a possible motive for killing Mary and, as far as he knew, the opportunity to try to drown her: both Pagets, Grundy, Paula Renton, and Winters.

But Mary Thornton hadn't been killed in Venice, she had died more than twenty-four hours later on the Orient Express. Just when had she swallowed the poison, drug, whatever it was that killed her? And how had she been induced to take it? Craig believed he knew the answer to the second question, and the French police should be able to help with the first.

The empty pill bottle had been worrying him, now he thought he knew how it had come to be in the bin in Mary's cabin. If he was right, the murderer was not only cold blooded, but clever and calculating too.

"Where have you been?" Muriel Grundy demanded as her son came into the room from the kitchen. "Why couldn't you tell me if you were going to be late? I didn't know what to do about supper." As usual, she hid her affection under a screen of antagonism. Only rarely did she let him see how she really felt.

"I went for a walk," Grundy replied. Her manner never deceived him. He wished he didn't feel both resentful of her affection, binding him as it did, and at the same time dependent on it.

"All this time?" Muriel grumbled. "A man came to see you."

"Who was it?"

"He said his name was Craig. He may come back this evening."

Grundy frowned. "Craig? What did he want?"

"*I* don't know. Something to do with your holiday, he said. I'm going to see to the potatoes." Suddenly Muriel didn't want to talk about Craig's visit. It had worried her, and after he left she had drunk two more glasses of sherry. Now she felt slightly muddled. Only her anxiety was clear.

"He didn't say anything?" Peter insisted.

Muriel took refuge in bad temper. "He asked a lot of questions about that girl. He wanted to know why you quarrelled in Venice."

"He's a private detective," Grundy said angrily. "What did you tell him?"

Muriel stared at him, "Nothing," she said. Then her resolution faltered. "Only . . . " What had she told him? She couldn't remember.

A private detective? she thought fearfully. He had said he knew the inspector in charge of the enquiries into Mrs. Adamson's murder. Why had he come here to see Peter?

12

THE incident room was at the rear of Fawchester's police station, an inconvenient Victorian building which had escaped closure and the transfer of its functions to the new divisional HQ at Lambsdown only because the local councillors argued that with so many houses in the town a prey to burglars the police should maintain a presence there. When Craig was shown in the room was crowded with men and women checking files, typing reports, and adding to the mass of accumulated information on three blackboards. He wondered how much of it would be of any help in tracking Ruth Adamson's murderer. But it had to be done.

Franklin was using a small office leading off the main room. He led the way to it and closed the door behind them.

"Have you changed your mind about telling us what you're doing here, or have you remembered something else you think we should know?" he asked, sitting down at his desk and regarding Craig with an unfriendly eye. Franklin was used to working long hours, but today had been frustrating, and he wasn't in the mood to listen to evasions and wild theories. His team had interviewed scores of people, taken as many statements and checked on dozens of known housebreakers. So far they had come up with nothing which seemed likely to solve the case quickly.

Craig took a chair facing him without being invited to. "I was hired by a man whose wife decided she fancied a man twenty years younger than herself," he said. "Her husband's twenty years older."

"What's her name?" Franklin demanded.

Craig shook his head. "It's nothing to do with your case."

They eyed each other without liking or hostility. In their way they were both professionals, and each recognised the other's position.

"All right," Franklin agreed. "But if I find it is, God help you."

"Have you contacted the French police?" Craig asked.

"It's in hand."

"You can't blame them for not busting a gut over what happened to Mary Thornton. She was a foreigner, on a train that was only passing through France, and everything pointed to suicide."

"I don't blame anybody," Franklin said. "I'm prepared to make an exception in your case though."

"What have I done?"

"You tell me. We've had a Ms." — the inspector's contempt was apparent in his tone — "Davidson come in. She says that Mrs. Adamson didn't like the Thornton girl and was talking in Venice about killing a character in one of her books. She thinks she may really have been thinking about Mary Thornton. Only she's sure Mrs. Adamson couldn't have killed anybody." Franklin paused.

"She says you told her to come."

"I just thought you should know," Craig said. He grinned. "It shows how public spirited I am."

Franklin looked unimpressed.

"Did she tell you she talked to Mrs. Adamson on the phone last night?" Craig asked him. "She could be the last person to speak to her."

"Could be. She wasn't."

"Who was?"

"The next-door neighbour, they chatted for a few minutes about nine-thirty. Your Ms. Davidson talked to her just after eight."

"I wasn't to know that," Craig objected. "Where was Mrs. Adamson when she was found?"

"I told you, halfway up the stairs."

"I know, but which stairs?"

"The back ones."

Craig experienced the sense of relief of one who finds a cherished theory proved right against all the odds. "They go up to the rooms Mary Thornton had," he said.

"What about it?"

"You said only one room had been disturbed. But if the murderer was coming down the stairs when they met, it looks as if he'd finished up there. Right?"

"Maybe."

"Was it her bedroom?"

"No, the living room."

"What did you find there?"

"One or two rings and necklaces. They were cheap stuff, he must have taken everything that was worth nicking, and left them."

"She didn't own anything valuable, she told Mrs. Adamson so. And if she had done, she'd have taken it with her to wear on the Orient Express."

"So?" Franklin's tone was sceptical, but he was listening attentively.

"An ordinary burglar would have gone for the downstairs rooms first," Craig said. "There were some good things there, silver and china. You said so yourself. Why did he ignore them and take the risk of going upstairs, then leave the few bits and pieces Mary Thornton had there?"

"Burglars do funny things, you know that."

"This one wasn't a pro, was he?"

"He may not have been."

"You know damn well he wasn't."

Franklin frowned. "What are you getting at?" he demanded.

"That Mary Thornton was murdered and the two crimes are connected. In a sense what happened to Mrs. Adamson was almost an accident, it wasn't planned. She was killed because she saw Mary Thornton's killer in her house, coming down from Mary's rooms, and she recognised him. Or her."

"You're trying to tell me he broke into her house because he wanted something the girl had in her room?"

"Yes."

"What evidence is there?"

"Some. All right, it isn't proof, but it fits." Craig paused, but Franklin didn't say anything, and he went on, "Several people on that trip didn't like Mary, but none of them seemed to have a strong enough motive for killing her. So it had to be something else. You ask anybody who knew her what she was like, and they'll tell you she was sly and nosy."

"'The evil that men do lives after them'," Franklin quoted unexpectedly. "It doesn't mean anything."

"It may do in her case," Craig said. "She was writing a history of Fawchester, and she'd done a lot of research for it. She'd filled two notebooks with stuff. Did you find them in her room?"

"No."

"Where are they then? She didn't take them to Venice, I heard her say so."

"How do I know? They could be anywhere." Franklin regarded Craig disgustedly. "We're dealing with a murder committed by a burglar, not history."

"You may have to deal with history," Craig told him. "I believe Mary Thornton had found out something about one of the Pagets' party, and they knew she had. Something that was so dangerous to them they tried to drown her out there, and when that failed they poisoned her on the train. But she hadn't got the notebooks with her, so whoever it was broke into Mrs. Adamson's house to look for them. Your 'burglar' wasn't interested in silver or porcelain, all he wanted was those two books."

"You call that evidence?" Franklin asked sarcastically.

"Where are the books?" Craig persisted. It was stalemate, he thought. Franklin wouldn't accept what he had told him, and he was convinced he was on the right track. "Look," he said, "there were twenty-two people in that party, not counting me, and nine of them came from here. Take out Mary and Ruth Adamson, and you're left with seven. When Mary was pushed into the canal one of those seven was in the bar, and another was with me. That leaves five unaccounted for."

"If you ask me, she killed herself," Franklin said.

"After she'd been in good spirits all day? Not the hectic, reckless sort, just ordinary good spirits. She was with

Winters, the sales manager at the brewery, part of the evening, and she looked all right then."

"Could he have killed her?"

"He could have done, but why should he? They hardly knew each other. She was probably just glad of his company after her row with Grundy."

"All right, maybe it was an accident. She'd had enough to drink to make her hazy about how many pills she was taking."

"She hadn't drunk much." Craig shifted on his chair. "There's a steward to each coach on the Orient Express. They're on call the whole journey, but it takes twenty-six and a half hours from Venice to Boulogne, and that doesn't take into account the time they're on duty before it leaves and after it arrives, so they grab sleep when and where they can. It's possible somebody slipped along the corridor to Mary's cabin during the night, but they'd have been taking a hell of a risk; somebody might have come out to go to the toilet at the end, or they might call the steward. Or the steward might be sitting on his seat at the end of the corridor all the time. Mary had been dead several hours when the doctor saw her; I reckon the poison was put into her orange juice during the evening so that she'd drink it before she went to bed. It seems to have been common knowledge that she was always drinking the stuff."

"Okay," Franklin said resignedly. "Let's say you're right, and she was murdered. Why couldn't it have been put in earlier?"

"Because she might have drunk some of the juice and passed out during the evening while she was obviously enjoying herself. Nobody would have believed it was suicide then.

"I'm not sure about the note. It's unlikely our man would risk going to her cabin during the night just to leave it. And if he did, he'd put it where it would be found straightaway. He may not even have known it existed, Mary may have put it in her pocket herself. But if he put it there, he must have chosen a jacket she wasn't likely to wear again that day so that she wouldn't find it before she went to bed." Craig stopped.

"Well?" Franklin demanded.

"The last one in to dinner that evening was Paget. And the one person we know for sure knew about the note is his wife. She says he didn't see it, but even if that's true, he probably knew it existed. Mary may even have given it to one of them to keep for the 'game'." Craig stood up. "I'm late for dinner."

"You're lucky to get any," Franklin told him. The phone on his desk rang and he picked it up.

Craig could hear a man's voice speaking.

When Franklin put the phone down his face was expressionless. "That was Brian Salisbury," he said. "Your friend Paget has scarpered."

Outside the rain had stopped and the wind had dropped. Fawchester, basking in the evening sunshine, looked its best. It was difficult to imagine anything evil happening anywhere so peaceful, so picturesque, and, above all, so respectable. It was an illusion, of course, evil existed here just as everywhere else. Not in dark, crumbling palaces, their stained walls rising from narrow, inky canals, but in whitewashed, half-timbered houses and modern, brightly lit shops.

Craig had said nothing to Franklin about Paula Renton. When he hinted to the colonel that he suspected he might obstruct the police to protect her he had meant no more than that. Nothing pointed to her as the murderer. Nothing except her manner that morning on the Orient Express. It had been as if, behind her facade of shock and grief, she was secretly relieved. Relieved that Mary was dead, or that everyone was taking it for granted that she had killed herself. She had even asked him if there was any doubt about that.

Craig was thankful that his job for the colonel was finished, his position might have been tricky if Mrs. Renton became a suspect and he was working for her husband.

She was supposed to be staying in Yorkshire when Ruth Adamson was murdered. Instead she was at an hotel not fifty miles from Fawchester. Moreover she and Winters had occupied separate rooms there; it would have been simple for her to slip out during the night, drive down here, kill Mrs. Adamson, and return to the hotel in the morning. Forcing the door at Church Cottage had required no skill, and almost certainly she possessed both the physical strength to beat an elderly woman to death and the resolution to go through with it. On the face of it it was absurd to suspect anyone like Paula Renton, and yet . . .

Why had Paget fled? Was it a signal of guilt, or merely the outcome of another row with Norma? Whatever the reason, he would soon be found, men like him had neither the mentality nor the aptitude to disappear successfully for long. Nor, generally, had they friends prepared to hide them.

Sue was looking out for Craig when he got back to the hotel. "There's a lady waiting to see you in the lounge," she said.

Craig sighed. He was hungry and fed up, he didn't like any part of this bloody business. But at least the woman couldn't be Betty Layton.

It wasn't, it was Leila. "They said you'd gone out before dinner," she explained. "I thought maybe we could eat together."

Her eyes met Craig's and he saw the familiar challenge in them. But this evening there was a defensive look too.

"Why?" he asked, hiding his pleasure at seeing her. "We always end up arguing."

"Blast you," Leila said. "I want company right now."

"Even a callous sexist's?"

She gave him a withering look and picked up her handbag. "Okay, maybe it wasn't such a good idea at that. Forget it."

Craig grinned. "You're always telling me what to do," he complained. "I don't want to forget it, I think it's a great idea."

"We — ell," Leila said. She smiled

happily. "That's different, I guess."

"I went to the police," she told him while they were waiting for the waiter to bring their pudding.

"I know," Craig said. "Franklin told me."

"You were right about him, he was okay." Demurely Leila added, "He doesn't approve of you."

"I could have told you that. How do you know?"

"The way he said 'Oh yes?' when I told him you'd said I should go."

"He has his reasons."

"I bet he has."

Craig drank the rest of the wine in his glass. It was a more expensive wine than he would normally have chosen, and he despised himself a little for wanting to impress Leila even in so small a thing. But perhaps it hadn't been that so much as self-defence, a gesture to show that he wasn't as skint as she might think. Anyway, his dinner was on the colonel, and Renton's fee would take care of the rest of the bill; he was damned if he was going to let Leila pay any of it.

"Mary Thornton didn't commit suicide," he said.

"She didn't?" Leila was startled. "I thought you said she did?"

"I've changed my mind."

"That's a woman's prerogative."

"Not in your brave new world it isn't."

"Okay, what made you?"

Briefly Craig told her.

"But why should anybody have wanted to kill her?" Leila asked.

"Because she knew something that the murderer couldn't afford to have come out," Craig replied. By now, he reflected, Mary's notebooks were probably ash, blown away by the wind or in somebody's dustbin.

What could she have discovered that was so dangerous to one of the Pagets' party? And how could the murderer know that she hadn't already talked about it to someone? Perhaps it wasn't something she had already discovered, but something she was certain to learn if she wasn't stopped.

But in that case, why take the risks inherent in breaking into Ruth Adamson's house to steal the notebooks? It seemed more likely that Mary had uncovered the secret and, not understanding its significance, had mentioned it to the person it most concerned.

Another idea occurred to Craig. Had she understood it very well, and tried to blackmail them? Was that the real meaning of those cheques to 'Cash' on Paula Renton's bank statement? If so . . .

Whatever the answer, one thing seemed clear, the secret lay in the past. Which meant that Winters, for one, could be eliminated as a suspect; he had only come to the district five or six months ago, and Craig couldn't see him sticking his neck out to protect anybody else. You could probably rule out the Pagets too, although they had lived in the town longer.

But cross them all off the list and you

were left with only two suspects, Paula Renton and Peter Grundy.

Without her notebooks there was no way of telling what, if anything, Mary had learnt, but at least, thanks to what she had said at dinner that evening and what Jane Baldwin, the librarian, had told him, Craig knew where she had done her research. Or rather, he would have done if he had paid more attention to what she was saying; at the time he hadn't been very interested in Mary's book.

"You remember when we had dinner at the same table as Mary and Clive Winters in Venice?" he asked Leila.

"Sure. I offended your masculine pride, and you got very English and huffy."

"I was cool and polite." Craig grinned.

"You were huffy," Leila said firmly. "What about it?"

"Do you remember where Mary said she'd been doing the research for her book?"

"Sure, the parish and county archives, a book some guy wrote years ago, and that place where they keep the births and deaths records."

"St. Catherine's House?"

"That sounds like it. Why?"

"I believe that while she was doing it she found out something about one of the people who were in Venice, and that's why she was killed."

Leila stared at him.

"Chocolate mousse for you, madam?" the waiter asked, coming to their table.

She looked up, and with a conscious effort concentrated on his question. "Yes, please," she said.

"Would you like cream with it, madam?"

"No, thanks." Leila wished the waiter would go away. What Craig said had shocked her.

"And gateau for you, sir," the waiter said.

"Yes," Craig agreed.

"Cream, sir?"

"Yes, please."

The waiter poured cream over the dark brown gateau and departed.

"Are you serious?" Leila demanded.

"Sure I am," Craig told her. "But what could she have found out?"

"I don't know. All that stuff's years old. Centuries, a lot of it. I can't see what she could discover that would be dangerous to anyone."

According to Jane Baldwin, Mary had spent a lot of time looking at back copies of the *Chronicle*, Craig thought. But that seemed no more likely a source than the others. Less likely indeed, for anything printed in a local newspaper became public knowledge within hours of its appearing. Unless, he told himself, it held some significance which only became apparent much later, when everybody had forgotten about it.

Of the people who could have murdered Mary Thornton, Paula Renton had the most to lose in a material sense, and the Rentons appeared more often in the *Chronicle's* columns than anyone else. Moreover Paula had known what Mary was doing.

Mary had said something else that

evening, Craig thought. What was it?

Later, when they were alone in the lounge drinking their coffee, Leila said accusingly, "You're looking very thoughtful."

"You want to know what I was thinking?" Craig asked, smiling broadly.

"Tell me."

"I was wondering what you'd do if I told you I fancied you."

"Hey, wait a minute!" Leila protested.

"It's all right, it wasn't a proposition. I just wondered what you'd say."

"You think that makes it better? It makes it a damn sight worse!"

"Okay then, I won't tell you."

"You know," Leila remarked coldly, "you're just about the most infuriating man I ever met, except my ex-husband. And he was just plain nasty."

"I didn't know you'd been married," Craig told her.

"I was nineteen, he was thirty-two. One of my teachers at college. It lasted all of two years. How was your marriage?"

"Great."

"For both of you?"

"Yes."

"What happened?" Leila's tone had changed.

"Jean was killed in a motor accident eighteen months ago."

"Oh. That was what you meant on the train when you said the death of somebody near to you was hard to accept, wasn't it?"

"Yes," Craig agreed.

For a minute neither of them spoke, then Leila said with unusual diffidence, "If you want to do something about what you didn't tell me, that's okay, I guess."

"Only okay?" Craig asked.

"All right; damn you;" Leila said. Her eyes were shining. "More than just okay."

The sun was shining and it was warm, but the girl Rosie looked as uninterested in life as she had done the previous day.

"I'd like to look at some more old

copies of the *Chronicle,*" Craig told her.

She slipped off her stool with a mumbled, "I'll get Mr. Gracie."

Craig wondered what, if anything, would relieve the blankness of her expression and bring her to something like normal life. Beside him on the wall there was a poster advertising a Grand Pageant Gymkhana held two years before, and he studied it until, after a minute or two, Rosie returned with the printer.

"How far back do you want to go this time?" the latter enquired warily.

"Twenty-five years," Craig told him.

"Twenty-five years!" Gracie gaped at him. Then he pulled himself together and the mercenary gleam returned to his eye. "That'll be another ten pounds."

"No," Craig said.

"You only paid for the one inspection before. This is another one. If you want to look, you'll have to pay."

Craig leaned so far across the counter that their faces were almost touching.

The printer had hairs growing out of his nose and ears, and his breath smelt unpleasantly. Rosie watched, blank faced as ever.

"Would you rather have me or the police? They'll swarm all over this place if you don't let me see those back numbers. And they won't pay you either."

Gracie gulped. "We have very good relations with the police," he gabbled. "We always have done. I'd give them any help I could."

"I'm sure you would," Craig agreed. "But it'll be easier if I look, wont it?"

"Why? Who are you? You aren't the police."

"I'm working for them."

"Oh well, that's different. Why didn't you say so? Then I'd have known." The printer managed to sound indignant. "You'd better come through."

Craig followed him into the big, musty smelling room behind the shop. Through the wall he could hear the old machinery in the print shop clattering busily.

"Twenty-five years ago's over there,"

Gracie said, nodding to indicate the far corner. He hesitated for a moment as if he were going to say something else, then went out, leaving whatever it was unsaid.

Craig set to work. The first reference he could find to Paula was the report of her engagement to Lieutenant Colonel Seymour Arthur Gervase Renton MC in May 1962. She was described as Miss Paula Jane Hesketh of Paris. According to the *Chronicle's* reporter, she had been living and working in France for the last two years and had met the colonel when he was in Paris on business six months before. Her home had been in Westmorland, but both her parents were dead.

A month later she and the colonel were married quietly in a small town near the French capital, and in July there was a photograph of them together taken soon after their return from their honeymoon. Renton was smiling stiffly, Paula, a little slimmer but instantly recognisable, radiantly.

After that there were frequent reports of their public activities, but nothing which could conceivably have any bearing on Mary Thornton's death. The Rentons, it seemed, had led a happy and blameless existence.

Craig went on working his way diligently through the binders. In a copy dated September 1966, he came across a report of the death of Mr. James Grundy, second master at Lambsdown Grammar School. Mr. Grundy, the *Chronicle* said, had been well-liked and respected, but then, Craig thought cynically, who wasn't in local rag obituaries? The teacher had left a widow and a son, Peter, 'both well known in the town'. The following week there was an account of the funeral.

So it continued, the endless reportage of trivial events, fêtes, cricket matches, and tennis in the summer, amateur drama and jumble sales in the winter. With only minor changes the *Chronicle* would be interchangeable with papers in the Midwest of America or the heart of the Soviet Union. And it told Craig nothing.

He began to think it never would. Already he had been there nearly three hours. Then, in the copy dated 23 August 1980, he saw something which brought him up short.

The report occupied a large part of the front page. Two days before a Miss Dorothy Waugh, an old lady who lived alone in a village near Fawchester, had been found dead in the sitting room of her cottage. It appeared that she had been poisoned. Miss Waugh was something of a recluse, and as far as was known her only living relative was a niece, an American, who had stayed with her recently. The niece, a Miss Leila Davidson, was understood to have returned to the U.S.A. a fortnight before the tragedy.

13

CRAIG stared at the report. Why hadn't Leila told him? Perhaps, he thought bitterly, she hadn't trusted him enough. He had once been a policeman, he wouldn't believe her.

But why should she tell him? Her aunt had died six years ago, her death was history.

With a dead feeling, he turned the pages. The next week's copy contained a lengthy report of the inquest. Miss Waugh had died as the result of swallowing much more than a lethal amount of a particularly deadly weed-killer. She had few friends and her neighbours saw her only occasionally, but as far as anyone knew she hadn't been depressed before her death. However she was forgetful and her eyesight was falling, it was possible that she had forgotten putting weed-killer in a green wine bottle and leaving it in her kitchen. The bottle on the table in her dining room amidst the dirty crockery and the remains of the old lady's dinner contained no wine, only the chemical, and in the absence of any evidence pointing to suicide the coroner's jury returned an open verdict.

Craig sat hunched over the table, gazing with eyes that didn't see at the page in front of him. The police had obtained a statement from Leila in America confirming her aunt's forgetfulness and that she was very short-sighted. She hadn't seemed to be depressed while she was staying with her. No, she knew nothing of the weed-killer, but the old lady was a keen gardener.

Craig resumed his search, and before long he found a brief paragraph on an inside page. It was headlined 'TRAGEDY VICTIM LEAVES FORTUNE TO NIECE'. Miss Waugh, the report said, had left over £150,000. After a few comparatively small bequests to charities, the residue had passed to

Miss Leila Davidson of Cookstown, Connecticut.

Could there be another Leila Davidson? No, Craig knew he would be deluding himself if he chose to believe that.

One hundred and fifty thousand pounds in 1981 would be worth at least a quarter of a million now, perhaps more; even after taxes and the other legacies that was still a great deal of money. Enough to enable Leila to work only sometimes, to travel pretty expensively, and to dress well.

Craig made himself consider the facts dispassionately, as if she were a stranger. Miss Waugh had drunk poison from a wine bottle, Mary Thornton in a bottle of orange juice. Leila must have had ample opportunities to put the weed-killer in the bottle, and she could have tampered with Mary's juice. Moreover she had known Ruth Adamson; it was a reasonable assumption that she had been in her house and knew which part of it Mary occupied. Added to all of which she was active and athletic, physically perfectly capable of striking the blows which killed Mrs. Adamson.

Physically. Craig steeled himself to go on. If Miss Waugh was murdered, her killer had displayed the same calculation and knowledge of his victim's habits as Mary's murderer had done. And he had chosen the same means, poison.

It was no good telling himself that Leila was psychologically incapable of murder, he was only too well aware that you had to know a person much better than he knew her to say that with any certainty. And even then you could be wrong.

Living alone as she did, she could easily have slipped out of her cottage and back again unobserved. And if Ruth met her coming down the stairs from Mary's old rooms, she would certainly have recognised her. Unless it was very dark. And it couldn't have been, or his whole theory collapsed.

Yesterday, like Paula Renton on the train, Leila had asked him if there was any question that Mary had killed herself and told him that story about Ruth Adamson's saying she was going to kill Francesca and her manner when she said it. According to her, Mrs. Adamson had claimed that Mary was following her everywhere. Had she made up all that to divert suspicion from herself? There was another thing, Ruth Adamson had phoned Leila the evening before she was murdered. Had she said something then which told Leila that the writer was a threat to her safety?

But what motive could Leila have had for killing Mary? Or for stealing her notebooks? Even if the dead girl had read the account of Miss Waugh's death, what would it have mattered? Any danger was over long ago. Unless Mary had discovered something else, either from these old files, or from her researches at St. Catherine's House. Something, perhaps, which had led her to attempt blackmail?

Craig had already toyed with the idea of going to St. Catherine's House, now he knew that he must.

Less than an hour ago he had been on the point of telling himself that the case was no concern of his, he should go back to London, get on with his own work, and forget it. No longer. Now he was involved. Who had killed those two women was very much his concern.

What was he doing? he asked himself wretchedly. Until he saw that damned report he had believed that one of four people, Paula Renton, Grundy, and the Pagets, was the murderer. Leila wasn't even a suspect. Now he was putting her near the top of the list. Why?

Because he was afraid, he thought. It was no good trying to convince himself that he should have faith in her and take her innocence for granted, that wasn't enough. He had to discover who had killed Mary and Ruth Adamson, however painful the knowledge might be.

Fired with a new determination, Craig read on. But after a few minutes he stopped again. All along he had assumed that it was Mary's killer who pushed her into the canal, and Leila had been with him then. She couldn't have pushed Mary.

A great weight was lifted from Craig's mind. But not for long. It was on the cards that Betty Layton was right, and Mary had jumped into the water, perhaps in a black, despairing moment, and nobody had pushed her. And by jumping she might have given somebody who hated and feared her the idea for killing her in such a way that it would be taken for granted that she had committed suicide.

Craig thrust the thought aside and resumed his reading.

By the time he decided to call a halt for lunch he had learnt no more. He told the girl Rosie that he would return at two-thirty, and walked up the street to the Golden Hart hoping fervently that Leila wouldn't be there today. When they parted this morning she had asked, "See you soon?" and he had replied, "If you want to."

"I do," she had told him. "Give me a call, Alan. Please."

He had promised that he would. It had all seemed so natural, almost inevitable.

Nothing Craig learnt from his third visit to the *Chronicle* offices that afternoon seemed likely to help him. The only further mention of Leila was a rather fulsome article when her last book was published. He returned to the hotel at five o'clock bleary eyed and stiff, and feeling as weary as if he had done a day's hard physical labour.

The next morning he paid his bill and drove back to London. He felt guilty about not calling Leila, but he didn't know what to say to her. Once this bloody business was cleared up it would be different.

Georgie was in her tiny office. After the affectations and evasions of some of the people he had encountered during the last few days her uncomplicated friendliness was a pleasant change. But there was something different about Georgie today, her hair had reverted to its usual dark brown. Moreover she had only one ring in each ear, and her make-up was almost conservative.

"'Allo," she greeted him. "You're back then." Georgie wouldn't have dreamed of welcoming Craig enthusiastically, but she was glad to see him all the same. She quite missed him when he was away. There was no one for her to spar with verbally, for one thing; Les wasn't the type, and Dave was out on site most of the time.

Craig eyed her hair and grinned. "You and Con had a row?" he enquired.

"Monday night," Georgie said disgustedly. "'E was a right pig. And 'e wasn't even Irish."

"What did I tell you?" Craig said. "You must keep your hairdresser in business."

"I get special rates, my sister works there. D'you want your coffee now?"

"Great."

Craig went into his office and switched on his recording machine. There had been only two calls while he was away, one from his bank asking him to get in touch with them, and the other from a firm of solicitors in the City for whom he had done work ocasionally. On the principle of hearing the bad news first, he rang the bank. The assistant manager said he thought Craig would want to know that his overdraft was £47.65 over the limit they had agreed last month, and would he please do something about it. Craig would much rather not have known, but he didn't say so, and he promised to pay something in during the next few days.

The solicitors weren't good news either, a girl clerk there said they wanted to query his last account. They had had it for over a month, Craig thought bitterly. And they were piddling bloody queries. He answered them all, told the girl he would be grateful if they would pay him now, and hung up.

He had just done so when Georgie came in with his coffee. Craig wondered sometimes whether his landlords knew that she brought him coffee in the mornings and tea in the afternoons every day when he was there, presumably at their expense. He had offered to pay when she first asked if he would like her to bring them, but she had brushed the suggestion aside with a casual, "That's all right," and after that he hadn't liked to press the point; it would have seemed too much like ingratitude. Perhaps, he thought, Les had allowed for tea and coffee in his rent. It was high enough.

When Craig had drunk his coffee he walked down to Fleet Street and along to St. Catherine's House at the corner of Aldwych and Kingsway. As usual it was busy with people trying to trace their family trees and others, professionals, armed with lists of names, working swiftly and methodically. Craig had been there several times before and he knew the ropes.

The registers at St. Catherine's House contain entries for all births, marriages, and deaths in England and Wales since 1837. There are supplementary records of deaths at sea and in the two world wars. The public have access only to the indexes to the registers, large volumes bound in red for births, green for marriages, and black for deaths, each of which covers a period of three months.

The Rentons had been married in June 1962. According to the colonel, his wife had been twenty-four then. If he was right, and while husbands didn't always know their wives' true ages, it was fairly unlikely that a girl of Paula Hesketh's age marrying a much older man would have lied about hers. She had been born between June 1937, and June 1938. Craig made for the shelves holding the indexes for births in 1937, found those for the second quarter, and took down the volume containing the H's. He wasn't sure what he hoped to find. Some discrepancy, perhaps. Something which pointed to a secret which Mrs. Renton might have been prepared to kill to preserve. It was well nigh hopeless, he knew, but he had to try. Thoughts of Leila haunted him.

And perhaps it wasn't so hopeless after all. If he was right, Mary Thornton had discovered something, or Mrs. Renton believed she would inevitably do so soon, and if she could, so could he. Craig wondered if there was any significance in the Rentons' having been married in France. Families like his would normally marry in England, either in the bride's home town or village or at some fashionable London church. Perhaps the colonel's having been married before had something to do with it, although he was a widower, not divorced.

Entries in the indexes aren't dated, nor necessarily in chronological order, so Craig had to check all those for the quarter ended 30 June 1937. He was thankful that Hesketh was an uncommon name, if Mrs. Renton had been born a Smith his task would have been impossible. As it was, there were only a handful of entries. He worked quickly, replacing each binder as he finished with it, and taking down the next, resting them on one of the high, sloping desks. Finally, because a birth during the last few days of one month might not be registered until the beginning of the next, he checked the third quarter of 1938.

The task didn't take him as long as he had feared, and he didn't need the notebook he had brought with him; only one Paula Jane Hesketh had been born during those eighteen months, and she had first seen the light of day some time in the autumn of 1937 in that part of Essex which loses its identity in the eastern suburbs of London.

Craig turned to the indexes of the marriage registers. He decided that he could safely eliminate any girls who had married before May 1962, when the Rentons became engaged — if and when they remarried their names wouldn't have been Hesketh — and go no farther back than the second quarter of 1953 when the oldest of them would have been only just sixteen. Even so, it was a fairly laborious process because it entailed his checking every index for those ten years. He found nothing. No Paula Hesketh had been married anywhere in England or Wales during that period. Which wasn't surprising, he thought, Mrs. Renton had been married in France, and there would be no record of her marriage in the English registers.

He walked round the room to where the indexes of the deaths registers were housed. Checking the entries here was an even longer task than tracing the marriages, for he had to go right back to the second quarter of 1937, but at last it was done: the only Paula Jane Hesketh to be born in England and Wales during those crucial eighteen months had died in that same district of Essex at some time in the first quarter of 1941, a victim, perhaps, of one of that winter's air raids on London. She had been three and a half years old.

He gazed at the brief entry. Was this what Mary Thornton had discovered? It was possible that Paula Renton had been born abroad, in one of the old colonies or dominions, perhaps. Or in Scotland or Northern Ireland. Craig was disinclined to believe it. There had seemed something very conclusive about the dying of the only child with that name in these registers. Mrs. Renton was a liar — and very likely something a great deal worse.

Mary couldn't have realised the implications, or she would hardly have talked about the older woman's kindness and the Rentons' family tree she was going to work on. It made no difference, Paula Renton must have known that it was only a matter of time. No wonder she had been worried and on edge.

Craig walked back to his office, dropping into a pub for some sandwiches and a pint of beer on his way. Georgie was still at lunch. He went into his room, sat down at his desk and made himself think coolly and logically about what he had learnt. If he was right, Leila was cleared of any suspicion. Not only her, but the Pagets, Winters, and Grundy too. If . . . It was all too flimsy, little more than an idea, a hunch, appealing, but with no firm evidence to support it. He was grasping at straws, and he could imagine what Franklin would say.

One thing, however, was certain, he needed the inspector's help. Picking up his phone, he dialled Fawchester police station and told Franklin that he was driving down to see him. Franklin didn't sound as if he felt that the news made his day, but he agreed that he would be there, and Craig hung up.

Walking round to retrieve his car, he told himself that he must find somewhere cheaper to park it, the multi-storey garage was costing him a bomb. He couldn't leave his car in the street any more, even with his home-made DOCTOR sign stuck up behind the windscreen; the traffic wardens nearly dislocated their jaws laughing and reached for their pads of tickets as soon as they saw it. Whoever first said that familiarity bred contempt didn't know how right he was.

It wasn't until he turned out into the street that Craig remembered that he hadn't started typing his report for the colonel. He hadn't done his account either.

"No!" Franklin said emphatically. "Even if her name wasn't Hesketh when she married Colonel Renton, that doesn't mean that she has a record."

"She must have applied for a passport in a false name."

"What about it? She may have changed her name legally, plenty of people do."

"It's the old racket," Craig insisted. The inspector's expression didn't change. "You mean you won't."

"That's right. You know what the chief constable would say if I did? That I was harassing the public because of some hairbrained theory without any evidence to back it up. People don't like having their fingerprints taken, you know that. It makes them feel like criminals, and they don't believe we destroy the prints if they're innocent."

"He'd probably praise your initiative," Craig said.

"Like hell he would! You don't know our CC."

"He's a friend of the Rentons, I suppose."

"I don't know if he is or not. I don't want to know; he's as straight as they come, and that hasn't anything to do with it." Franklin saw Craig's expression and told himself that this case was difficult enough without amateurs who thought they were Sherlock Holmes coming and telling him what he should do. Only Craig wasn't an amateur, and he had been right once before. The inspector drew a deep breath. "Look," he said, "the Rentons are important people round here. They have been for several hundred years."

"You mean, you'd do it if it was me," Craig said.

"Too true I would."

"But not one of them. Christ, how I hate places like this!"

"You don't understand them. You don't want to. I was born and brought up here. A lot of people in towns like

327

this like things to be a bit old-fashioned. It gives them a sense of continuity, and makes them feel secure. It's about the only thing that does these days, God help them. You might say it bolsters their idea of their place in the order of things. A lot of the people who've moved in are either new middle class, or clinging on to their middle-class existence by their fingertips, and it suits them to have a family like the Rentons living at the big house. They've worked for what they've got, most of them, and they aren't necessarily snobs. There are a lot of people like that. And not just in Britain either. Most of them are all right. I'll tell you this, two of the most respected men in Fawchester are Tom Shaw and George Day; Tom's a cleaner at the school and George works for Geesons. He's a carpenter. They're known and liked as individuals, not units in some bloody survey. Can you say that about people where you live?"

"All right," Craig agreed; impressed despite himself. "So you won't do it?"

"No. You know as well as I do, there are people who can make real trouble if you overstep the mark. They know how to go about it, and the right people to talk to. It's nothing to do with class, and it's the same everywhere, London, New York, probably Moscow too. I'm not saying Colonel Renton would make trouble, he's probably less likely to than a lot of other people, but I'm not prepared to take the risk for some crazy idea of yours."

"And if she murdered those women?" Craig asked.

"You bring me real evidence, and I'll change my mind. It won't make a ha'p'orth's difference who she is then."

"Tell them you're taking the prints of everybody who was in the Pagets' party for elimination purposes."

"Who am I supposed to be eliminating? Mary Thornton?"

Their eyes met.

"Let them know her death is linked with Mrs. Adamson's," Craig suggested. "It can't do any harm. Have you heard from France yet?"

"Yes," Franklin replied. "They say she died from a larger than fatal dose of a barbiturate almost certainly taken in her orange juice. And she'd been drinking earlier. Not a lot, but enough to enhance the effect of the drug, even if there hadn't been enough to kill her anyway. They're satisfied she committed suicide."

"Who wouldn't be in their position?" Craig asked. Mary had said she didn't like wine, he thought, but that didn't mean she didn't drink spirits. And she had been happy that evening. "I've been wondering about the empty pill bottle in her waste-paper bin," he said. "If the murderer dropped it in there after he'd put the drug in her orange juice, she would have remembered it wasn't there before when she dropped the tissues on top of it. That might have made her suspicious. But he couldn't take it away with him — or she couldn't with her — because if Mary had killed herself, she wouldn't have bothered about getting rid of it."

"So what did he do with it?" Franklin wanted to know. "You say it was there when you went to her cabin."

"He left it in a corner, or under the table. If you found a little bottle there, you'd think that the last person to have your cabin dropped it, it had rolled out of sight, and the cleaner had missed it, right?" The inspector nodded. "You'd pick it up and put it in the waste-paper bin. I reckon that's what Mary Thornton did."

"The cunning bastard," Franklin said. "All right, I grant you it's possible she was murdered — possible, I say — but the odds are still on Mrs. Adamson's having been killed by an intruder who broke in to see if she had anything worth nicking."

"That would make everything nice and cosy, wouldn't it?" Craig said.

"Look — "

"Have you found Paget yet?"

"No. We will."

"I don't think he did it."

"Why not?"

Craig decided that the time had come when he must tell Franklin what had brought him to Fawchester in the first place. "It was your Colonel Renton hired me," he said.

"The colonel?" Franklin looked as if he found that hard to believe. "You said it was an old man who — "

"He was concerned about his wife, she'd been worried and on edge for some time and she wouldn't tell him what was wrong. I think he was afraid she was being blackmailed."

"Go on."

"One of the people who went to Venice was Clive Winters, the sales manager at the brewery here. It struck me that it was a bit odd his going, he was the only young guy there and he was on his own. Then one of the others hinted that he and Mrs. Renton were having a bit on the side. Last Saturday Mrs. Renton went away for two or three days. She told Mrs. Adamson she was going to Yorkshire, but it was a lie, she stayed at a hotel in Kensington. Winters was there too, he was supposed to be on a sales trip." Craig paused. "I told you it hadn't anything to do with your case. Once I'd reported what I'd learnt to Renton, that was the end of it as far as I was concerned. I went back to London this morning."

"So what brought you back?"

Craig met Franklin's look squarely. "I think Mrs. Renton killed Mary Thornton and Ruth Adamson," he answered.

"Go on," the inspector said again, grimly. Craig explained.

When he had finished there was a lengthy silence in the little room. Outside in the yard a policeman called to a colleague. A van's door slammed metallically, and farther off an ambulance went down the High Street, its siren wailing.

"All right," Franklin said at last. "I'll take all their prints, starting with yours. But I tell you, I don't like it, and you'd better be right."

If he wasn't, Craig thought, Leila would be back near the top of the list of suspects. He hadn't mentioned her to Franklin.

Ten minutes later when he emerged from the police station she was coming out of the Golden Hart. He stopped. It was clear that she had seen him too, and for a second they gazed at each other across the width of the street. By now she would have learnt that he had booked out of the hotel this morning, Craig told himself. She was bound to think that for him the other night had been no more than an enjoyable interlude, and that he had never had any intention of calling her. Instead, shamefully, he had slipped away back to London.

It would have been impossible for him to avoid her now, even if he had wanted to do so. To turn and walk away as if she hadn't been there. And there was no reason why he should. He started to cross the street. At the same moment Leila took a step towards him, and they met at the edge of the pavement.

"They told me you'd gone," she said with a brightness that carefully avoided any hint of accusation.

"I booked out this morning," Craig told her.

"Are you going back to London?"

"I'm backwards and forwards. I haven't finished here yet."

"Oh." Leila's cool grey eyes searched Craig's face.

"I've been up to my eyes the last two days."

"Yeah."

Craig knew she didn't believe him, and he wondered if other men besides her husband had let her down in the past. He wanted to explain, to ask her why she hadn't told him about her aunt's death and how it was that she lived in England, but he couldn't bring himself to do it. His fear was a barrier between them.

"I've had to read through the back numbers of the *Chronicle* for the last twenty-five years," he said, thinking that by telling her he was giving her an opportunity to explain without his asking her.

But Leila merely looked puzzled. "Have

335

you?" she said. It sounded like an accusation.

"Then I had to go up to Town this morning to do some checking there." Her lack of response and his own guilty conscience were forcing him to excuses for which he despised himself. Since Jean died his relationships with women had been casual on both sides; he hadn't much cared what they thought of him, because he knew that nothing between them would last. Why should it be different now?

Leila saw his evasiveness, and disappointment, humiliation, and anger swelled up in her. Who did he think he was to treat her as if she were some hooker he had picked up in a bar the other evening? But he hadn't picked her up, she had made the running all the way, ever since their first meeting in Venice. She had as good as hijacked him into going with her in the gondola that evening, when it was clear he hadn't wanted anything to do with her. Was her behaviour supposed to make her proud? To demonstrate that she was a truly liberated woman? If so, she had failed miserably; he despised her, and she despised herself.

Craig saw only his own feelings of guilt and fear. "Let me just finish this job," he pleaded. "It won't be long now."

"Sure," Leila agreed brightly. "Give me a ring some time if you want to. 'Bye, Alan."

She strode off down the hill without looking back. Craig watched her go.

14

THE next day was Friday, and it was four days before Craig heard from Franklin. Georgie had just brought him his coffee when the phone rang. He put down his cup, picked up the phone and said, "Alan Craig Associates."

"Craig? Franklin. We took all their prints. You were right, she has a record." The inspector sounded like a man who had received some bad news and held Craig responsible for it.

"Did she object?" Craig asked.

"No. The colonel wasn't there. When I explained what I had come for she looked upset and asked if it was really necessary. I told her it was, and she said, very well, she must then. She seemed sort of resigned, as if she'd been expecting it."

"She probably had."

"Christ, it was nearly thirty years ago!"

"Before she was married."

"That's another thing," Franklin said. "The colonel's her second husband."

"*What?*" Craig exclaimed. "I asked the colonel if she'd been married before, and he said she hadn't."

"I shouldn't think he knows. Her first husband was a villain named Terry Benson; she married him when she was eighteen. In 1958 he and a man named Findlay did a jeweller's in Golders Green. They were carrying guns. They didn't use them, but Benson got nine years and Findlay seven. She was the driver. She claimed that Benson had asked her to take them to the shop and wait while they picked up a retirement present for the steward at a club they belonged to. According to her, she had no idea what they were really going there for, but nobody believed her, and she got three years. She came out in 1960, and disappeared."

"She didn't disappear," Craig said. "She got herself a passport in the name of Paula Jane Hesketh and went to

France." Perhaps she had told the truth at her trial, he thought, and she hadn't known what her husband and Findlay were going to do at the jeweller's. But you couldn't blame the jury for not believing her: she was Benson's wife, she must have known that he was a crook and how he made the money they lived on. Suspected, at the very least. "What was her maiden name?" he asked.

"Pamela Mary Andrews. She was born in a little place called Welburton in Leicestershire. Her father died, and when she was seventeen she went to live in London."

"Do you know where she and Benson lived after they were married?"

"Romford. That's where they were arrested."

Romford was where Paula Jane Hesketh was born, Craig reflected. And where, three and a half years later, she had died. Had Pamela Benson known the Heskeths and later, just released from prison and anxious to start a new life, remembered hearing about little Paula, who would have been near enough her own age if she had lived? Or had she searched the local cemeteries for a child's grave and stumbled by accident on that of Paula Jane? Whichever it was, she must have applied for a copy of the little girl's birth certificate and used it to obtain a passport. Then, provided with a new identity, she had made a fresh start in France. Two years later she had met Renton and married him, taking herself another big step away from Pamela Benson, crook's wife and ex-convict.

As time passed she must have become increasingly confident that her secret was safe. She was happily married and respected. Then Mary Thornton had started probing into the Rentons' history and announced that she wanted to bring the family tree up to date.

"You think the Thornton girl discovered that there was no genuine Paula Jane Hesketh of the right age?" Franklin enquired.

"No," Craig replied. "I don't think she'd got that far. But Mrs. Renton couldn't be sure she hadn't, anyway, it was only a matter of time before she did."

"All right, she had a motive. I'll give you that," Franklin conceded. He paused. "They say leopards can't change their spots, but whatever she did before, for the last twenty-odd years she's done everything right."

"Until now," Craig said.

Franklin had a point, he thought. All the same, Paula Renton had been living a lie, and eventually it had caught up with her. He should have derived some satisfaction from being proved right, but somehow he didn't.

He knew that the inspector was telling himself that there was nothing like enough evidence yet to charge her with either murder, and wondering what his chief constable was going to say about it all. They might prosecute her for obtaining a passport by deception. But even that was unlikely after all this time, taking into account her apparently blameless life until Mary Thornton and Winters came on the scene.

"She isn't the only one with a record," Franklin said.

Craig felt a touch of fear. "Who's the other?" he asked as casually as he could.

"Paget. Five years ago he assaulted a young woman he was having it off with. It was before he and his wife came to Fawchester. The girl was well-known locally, notorious, you might say, and it looked as if there might have been provocation. It was his first offence, apart from a couple of tickets for speeding, and he got off with twelve months suspended."

Craig wondered if that was why Paget had fled now. He had told Norma about the possibility of Mary Thornton's being murdered to see her reaction. He hadn't expected this. Norma must have stood by her husband five years ago, no wonder she was angry and bitter if she found out that he was playing around with Mary Thornton.

"Has there been any sign of him?" he enquired.

"Not yet," Franklin admitted. "But we'll find him. If it wasn't a burglar, I still reckon he did it. His wife thinks so too, she's worried stiff. I can't see your favourite breaking into Mrs. Adamson's, creeping round looking for a couple of notebooks, and battering her head in when she disturbed her."

Because you don't want to, Craig thought. But all he said was, "Where are the notebooks then?"

"They could be anywhere."

"Mary was working on them, she'd have kept them by her handy. And I can't see there being anything about Paget in them, he's only lived in Fawchester three or four years. Have your people searched the house?"

"They've gone through the whole place with a fine-tooth comb," Franklin said bitterly. "The books aren't there."

They talked for a minute or two longer, then Craig put down his phone. What the inspector had told him didn't answer all the questions. Indeed, it raised several new ones.

For some time Craig sat at his desk deep in thought.

The next morning's post brought two circulars, one bill and a cheque from Colonel Renton. There was no accompanying letter with the cheque, and Craig guessed that for the old man it had been a point of honour to settle his account by return. He wouldn't have wanted to be indebted to him, of all people, and perhaps he had felt that by paying his bill promptly he was putting the whole distasteful business behind him. If so, he was mistaken. There was no way the colonel could dismiss what had happened, it would be with him for the rest of his life.

Just before ten Franklin phoned. "They were never divorced," he said. "And Benson's still alive, he's doing eight years for conspiracy to rob. I can't understand why she never divorced him."

"She had to describe herself as single

when she applied for a passport because she couldn't provide a marriage certificate for Paula Hesketh," Craig told him. "And afterwards she daren't divorce him; she was Paula Hesketh, not Pamela Benson, and she couldn't go back to her old name. Anyway, divorce wasn't so easy in those days."

"Is there anything else?" Franklin asked.

"I don't think so. Not at this stage. I may give you a ring later."

They said goodbye. Craig locked his office and walked across the landing to where Georgie, looking bored, was sorting invoices in her cubbyhole.

"You want coffee early this morning?" she enquired hopefully.

"No thanks, I shan't be here," Craig told her. "Georgie, can you let me have twenty quid?"

"Twenty?" Georgie looked slightly shocked.

"I've got to go up to Leicestershire, and I haven't time to go to the bank first."

"I 'aven't got twenty. Not of me own.

An' if I took it out of the petty cash, Les'd do 'is nut."

"I just want you to cash a cheque for me," Craig said. "That's all."

"Oh." Georgie still looked uncertain. She'd like to help Craig, but if the cheque bounced, Les would be right nasty.

"It's all right, I got paid for a job today. I'll put it in the bank tomorrow."

"Oh, that's okay then." Georgie wasn't a good dissembler and her relief showed. "I'll trust you, thousands wouldn't."

"Too right," Craig agreed with feeling. "No one trusts anybody these days."

Who was he to talk about trust? he thought dejectedly. He hadn't even trusted Leila. Already it was five days since that awkward, unsatisfactory encounter in the street; she would think he didn't want to see her again. And he did. But not while this business was like a distorting mirror between them, reflecting truth as deceit and understanding as suspicion.

He made out a cheque and took the two ten pound notes Georgie gave him in exchange for it. "You're a darling," he told her.

"That's what you all say when you want something," Georgie retorted. "Men!"

Craig forebore to ask what men wanted from her and, grinning, ran down the stairs and round to the car-park.

It took him longer than usual to negotiate the North London traffic, but once he was on the M1 he pressed his foot down. The old Triumph responded gallantly, but as usual north of Watford sections of the motorway were partially closed for repairs and there were the inevitable delays. Craig pushed a cassette into the stereo unit and relaxed to a Judy Collins tape while the traffic ground along in the two remaining lanes.

Welburton turned out to be a tiny village at the junction of two lanes just to the west of the M1. Once the area had been part of Sherwood Forest, and it was still well wooded with oaks and beeches. Craig drove along the street slowly, looking for a pub. In a place like Welburton the local pub and the post office were the most likely sources of the sort of information he wanted, and it was just after twelve-thirty. At that time a pub should be pretty busy.

The first one he came to, the Axe and Compasses, was a low stone building, scrupulously maintained, with flowerbeds full of geraniums, and a renovated farm cart, its shafts pointing to the sky, standing on the triangle of grass between the pub and the road. Craig saw the large car-park, already nearly full of Fords and Vauxhalls with the odd Volvo and BMW, and drove on. They were reps' and managers' cars, and he guessed that most of the Axe and Compasses' lunchtime customers came out from offices in the nearest towns. He would learn nothing he wanted to know from them, and the landlord would be too busy to talk. In any case, he was probably a manager put in by the brewery a year or two ago, and he would know nothing.

The Hoops, seventy yards farther on on the other side of the street, was a very different pub, a beerhouse with few pretensions to being anything else. The plaster on its walls was holed in places, revealing the laths behind, and its woodwork sorely needed repainting. In one of the windows there was a crooked sign, PUB FOOD. It was fly-blown, and seemed unlikely to instil confidence in any prospective customer. Across the road the few square yards of dust and gravel which served the pub as a car-park were deserted except for a rusty wheelbarrow minus its wheel, a battered oil drum, and a brown and black mongrel which watched suspiciously as Craig got out of his car but didn't move.

The door of the Hoops opened straight into the only bar, a low room with stained walls whose only decorations were two ancient photographs of the village and a picture of the Queen which looked as if it had been there since her coronation in 1953. The air was thick with tobacco smoke, and from a table in one corner came the hard clink of dominoes. There were about a dozen men in the room. No women; Craig couldn't imagine any woman wanting to drink in a place like this. The customers had stopped talking and were eyeing him in much the same way as the dog had done.

Craig walked up to the bar. The landlord, a burly, stooped man, was leaning on it, watching him impassively. He must be seventy, Craig thought. Maybe his luck was in.

"What food have you got?" he enquired.

"Sandwiches. They're all we do." As clearly as any words, the landlord's tone said, "Take it or leave it."

Craig took it. "What sort?" he asked.

"Cheese or cheese and tomato. There may still be a bit of 'am left."

"A round of cheese and tomato and a round of ham, if there is any then, please," Craig said. "And a pint of bitter." He had learnt long ago that in pubs like the Hoops the food was an uncertain quantity, to say the least, and tomatoes could improve dry mousetrap cheese to a point where it was just about eatable.

The landlord went out by a door at the back of the bar, to return almost immediately with the information that there was still some ham, and that would be £1.95. Craig paid him and sipped his beer. A sentimental man might have expected it to be better than that at the Axe and Compasses; Craig, from bitter experience, was prepared for it to be bad. He was right. Clearly the Hoops' customers didn't come here for the ale. Perhaps it was sheer bloody mindedness. And by now they had probably forgotten how bad the beer was; you could get used to almost anything in time.

Gradually, like a part song, the talk started again, at one table first, then the others following.

"It's a nice village," Craig remarked to the landlord.

"Ah, Welburton's all right."

"You been here long?"

"Thirty-nine years." There was a trace of pride in the old man's tone.

Thirty-nine years, and the Hoops was probably a worse pub now than when he came; it didn't seem much to be proud of,

Craig thought. He took another cautious sip of his beer.

"Did you ever know some people called Andrews here?" he enquired casually.

"Ol' Mrs. Andrews, you mean?" The landlord rested one brawny forearm on the bar counter. "Margaret 'er name was. She died four, five years back."

"There was a daughter, Pam. She went to live in London."

"Oh 'er." It was clear that the old man had a poor opinion of Pamela Andrews. "Are you interested in them then?"

"They're sort of cousins of mine," Craig said. Go far enough back, he thought, and it must be true.

A little old man even more bent than the landlord came up to the bar and pushed two empty pint glasses across its worn surface without speaking. He looked as if he might have been coming to the Hoops and drinking the same beer for sixty years and there was no longer any need for him to say what he and his companion wanted.

"This gen'leman's asking about Mrs.

Andrews an' that daughter of 'ers, Pam," the landlord told him, working the beer pump.

"Ah." The little man wiped his mouth with one cuff of his worn tweed jacket and his eyes brightened. "Ran away to London when she was seventeen, Pam did. She warn't no good. Married some crook down there. She warn't of age, an' 'er mother didn't like it, but Pam could always twist 'er round 'er little finger. Lot o' good it did 'er, though, by all accounts, she an' 'er 'usband both went inside soon after. 'E were a burglar or something, so they said, an' she 'elped 'im. Upset 'er mother terrible."

"Did she ever come back here?" Craig asked.

"Not that I 'eard of. Good as disappeared." The old man paid for his beer and carried the refilled glasses back to the table where his friend was waiting.

"Are any of the family still here?" Craig asked the landlord.

"Mrs. Andrews died a few years back,

like I said. An' Gwen, Pam's older sister, she went eighteen months ago. Brian, 'er 'usband's still 'ere, 'e lives just up the road there, in the big 'ouse with two gables. That was the Andrews' 'ouse when the old man were alive. Brian's a schoolmaster, 'ead of a big school in Leicester."

A short, stout woman brought Craig his sandwiches. They had little in common with the delicacies served at the Golden Hart, he thought, they were thick, dry, and unadorned with anything, and he tackled them without enthusiasm or hope.

"Nice bit of 'am that," the landlord observed complacently. "If you're wanting to see Brian, 'e'll be at 'is school now."

Craig, trying to chew a mouthful of tough and tasteless supermarket ham, nodded. It was going to be a long wait.

15

IT was past six when Craig got back to his office. Georgie had gone home some time ago, and her cubbyhole across the landing was in darkness. He went into his room, picked up the phone and dialled Colonel Renton's number.

"This is Craig," Craig told him when the colonel answered. "I'd like to speak to Mrs. Renton."

"Why?"

"I can't tell you that without her say-so."

"What do you mean, you can't? She's my wife. And I hired you."

"That's right," Craig agreed. "Hired. I don't work for you any longer. May I talk to her?"

There was a pause before the colonel answered, his reluctance clear over the phone, "Very well. Hold on."

Craig wasn't happy. Hurting people

gave him no pleasure, and he knew that what he was going to do would inevitably cause pain. But perhaps it would be easier, coming from him.

"Hallo? Mr. Craig?" Paula said.

"Yes. I want to see you, as soon as possible. Alone."

Craig sensed her fear as she said in a withdrawn voice, "I'm afraid that's out of the question. Colonel Renton told you to forget what you'd found out. I have nothing to say to you."

"You may not have, but I have something to say to you." Impatience and dislike of what he was doing made Craig's tone rougher than he had intended.

"What do you mean?" Paula demanded, echoing her husband. Despite her effort to speak coolly, she couldn't keep her apprehension out of her voice.

"I can't tell you on the phone. I'm coming down to Fawchester now; I'll be at your house in an hour and a half."

"No!"

"Don't you think you should know what you're up against?"

"If you think you can get money from me, or from Colonel Renton — "

"I'm not interested in your money," Craig said harshly. "And you're not in a position to be insulting."

"I'm sorry, I didn't mean . . . What is it then?"

"I'll tell you when I get there." "Do you have to be so mysterious?"

"Yes."

There was a brief silence. "Very well, if you must come," Paula agreed wearily.

Craig replaced his phone, then picked it up again and spoke to Franklin.

It was dark when he rounded the bend at the top of Fawchester High Street. Lights glowed orange-red against the night sky, and here and there a shop sign made a garish splash of colour, but most of the buildings were in darkness. Only the forecourt of the garage at the top of the street blazed with fluorescent light. Craig remembered that the Triumph's tank was three-quarters empty and pulled in beside the nearest pump.

Ahead of him a man was filling up an Escort XR3i. There seemed something familiar about his back, but he was stooped over, and it was only when he straightened up and half turned to replace the hose in its cradle that Craig saw it was Winters. The sales manager recognised him at the same moment.

"Hallo, Alan," he said amiably. "You're a long way from home, aren't you?"

"A fair distance," Craig agreed. "I've had a job here."

"Oh?" Winters smiled. "No use my asking what sort of job. You wouldn't tell me, would you?"

"No."

"I've been up to Town for a few days seeing customers. That's probably why I haven't seen you around."

"Could be," Craig agreed. The figures on the dial clicked up to £9.97 and he stabbed in three short bursts to bring them to the round £10. "You're back here now then?"

"Yes. I shan't be going again for

another two or three months."

Winters waited while Craig replaced the Triumph's filler cap, and they walked over to the cashier's window together. As they turned away after paying he asked, "Are you staying here?"

"I don't know. It depends how things turn out."

"How about a drink later?"

"All right."

"The Golden Hart? Nineish?"

"Okay." Casually Craig asked. "Have you seen any of the Venice crowd since we got back?"

"One or two. Why?"

"No reason. I heard about Mrs. Adamson."

"Yes. Bloody awful business." Winters opened his car's door and slid behind the wheel. Through the half-open window he said, "See you later then."

"Yes," Craig agreed.

When had Winters last spoken to Paula Renton? he wondered as he followed the silver-grey Ford out of the forecourt. He had shown no sign of knowing what he had been doing here.

Winters turned right, away from the town, and Craig drove down the High Street. The library was closed, and across the street a trick of the light casting a shadow of the Golden Hart's hanging sign on the cobbles made it seem for a moment as if the gibbet still stood there with some poor wretch suspended from it.

The brewery buildings were silhouettes behind their tall iron gates. Taking the right-hand fork at the bottom of the hill, Craig climbed the shoulder of the Downs and turned off along the drive to Fawchester Court. Through the gap at the end of the trees he could see lights on in the house.

His ring was answered by a comfortable looking woman in a gray dress.

"I'm Alan Craig," he told her. "Mrs. Renton's expecting me."

"Oh yes, sir." The woman's voice had a pleasant West Country burr. "Will you come this way?"

She showed him into a small room off

the hall and left him. Craig just had time to study a print of a three-masted warship in a rough sea before she returned and said, "Mrs. Renton can see you now, Mr. Craig."

He followed her along the hall to a room overlooking the terrace, although the long, heavy curtains at the french windows were drawn to exclude the autumn evening, and the only light came from two standard lamps. Paula wasn't alone. She and her husband had been sitting at opposite sides of the big fireplace, but when the housekeeper came to say that Craig was there the colonel had stood up and taken a position slightly in front of his wife and to her right, as if to protect her. They eyed Craig in silence, Renton glowering angrily, Paula looking pale and strained.

"What's all this about, Craig?" the colonel demanded as soon as the door had closed behind the housekeeper. "Why do you want to see Mrs. Renton?"

Craig ignored him. Speaking directly to Paula, he said, "I told you I needed

362

to see you alone, Mrs. Renton. It was for your sake."

"There's nothing you can't say in front of me," the colonel told him angrily.

"Is that true, Mrs. Renton?"

Paula moved slightly and the light shone directly on to her face. She had aged noticeably since Craig last saw her at close quarters, but although she couldn't conceal the fear in her eyes, she had herself well under control.

Renton didn't let her answer. "I employed you to do a job," he said, controlling his anger with difficulty. "I didn't pay you to harass my wife or me."

"That's right," Craig agreed. "I let you talk me into taking on a job I didn't want. I told you at the time I didn't like it, and I like it even less now. But you aren't paying me any longer, Colonel. You told me, as far as you were concerned, I'd finished."

"What do you mean?"

"I've told my husband everything," Paula said desperately. "Nothing you say can make any difference, why don't you go away and leave us alone? I know it wasn't your fault, but you've done enough damage already."

"The colonel knows what we've told him," Craig said roughly. "Both of us. And it isn't true. The only difference is that I thought it was; you fooled me just like you fooled him and everybody else. Do you still want him to hear what I'm going to say?"

Paula's shoulders sagged, and she didn't answer. It was her husband who said, "For God's sake tell him 'Yes.' There's been too much damned secrecy all along."

"Very well," Paula muttered.

Craig shrugged. "Has Winters been blackmailing you?" he asked.

"No!"

"But he's taken money from you every month?"

"I gave it to him because I wanted to." Paula raised her head to face Craig directly, and he was shocked by her eyes. They seemed to have sunk back into her skull, all life gone out of them. "I know what you think of me," she said.

"You don't," Craig told her.

Paula frowned uncertainly. "You told my husband that Mary Thornton was murdered. Why? it wasn't true. You said yourself on the train that there was no question she killed herself. That she'd left a letter saying why."

"I didn't know things then I know now," Craig told her.

"He says the same person killed her as killed Ruth Adamson," Renton said. "For God's sake, why don't you tell him you had nothing to do with it. You didn't."

The colonel was scared, Craig thought. Principally for his wife, but also, through her, for himself.

"I didn't," Paula almost whispered. "I was with Clive the night Ruth was murdered."

"All that night?" Craig asked.

Again she raised her eyes to meet his, and there was a note of defiance in her voice when she answered, "Yes."

"I don't believe you, Mrs. Renton."

The colonel's anger returned. "Are you accusing Mrs. Renton of lying?" he demanded furiously.

They took no notice of him. It was as if they were engaged in a deadly private duel, and nobody else had any part in it.

"You weren't with Winters that night," Craig said. "You aren't lovers, you never have been. That charade at the Crosslands was intended to be an alibi."

Paula gazed at him, unable to look away. "Why should I want to kill either of them?" she asked.

"Mary because of what she knew, or would know soon, about you, and Ruth Adamson because you had to get hold of Mary's notebooks in case there was something about you in them, and Ruth recognised you when she found you in her house."

"Oh, my God!"

Renton looked like a man torn between conscience and his own inclinations. "Go on," he growled.

"No, Arthur," Paula pleaded. "No! Please."

"You know why the police took your fingerprints, don't you?" Craig asked her.

"Yes," she whispered.

"I wondered why, if you weren't having an affair with Winters, you let people think you were. You even admitted it to the colonel. That might have meant the end of your marriage and your whole life here, and I think they both mean a lot to you, but even that was better than having people know the truth. Because that would have meant the end of this life anyway, and you'd probably go to gaol. There was another reason too, wasn't there?"

"Mrs. Renton's told me all about her life before we met," Renton said with a return of his former aggression. "I know she was married to a man who went to gaol for robbery. I know she was in prison too, for something she knew nothing about, because of him. It makes no difference. We've been married for over twenty years. I know what they've been like for me, and what we mean to each other. That's all I care about, and if you try to . . . "

He stopped, an old, shattered and frightened man. His left hand was by his side, close to the arm of his wife's chair, and she reached out to grasp it. Whether the gesture was instinctive, or intended as a sign of gratitude or a plea for support, Craig couldn't tell. It might even have been made for his benefit.

"I wanted to talk to Mrs. Renton alone, but you wouldn't have it," he said. "What she's done has put other, innocent people under suspicion, and now you have to face the consequences. Both of you." He turned to Paula. "Does the colonel know everything?"

"Everything?" she repeated dully.

"Do you want me to spell it out?"

"Go on," Renton said again grimly. "We may as well hear all you have to say now."

Craig was still looking at Paula. All the spirit seemed to have been drained out of her.

"What difference does it make?" she

asked hopelessly.

"Your real name's Pamela Benson," Craig said. "Your husband, Terry Benson, is a crook. He's still alive, and you've never been divorced. When you 'married' the colonel you committed bigamy, and legally he isn't your husband."

Renton was staring at his wife. "I don't believe it," he muttered.

"It's true, Arthur." Paula was crying. "I couldn't tell you. I couldn't. Oh God, if you knew how sorry I am!"

"Paula Hesketh was a little girl whose home had been near where you and Benson lived in Romford," Craig went on. "She died when she was three."

"She was killed in the blitz," Paula said.

"When you came out of prison you wanted to start a new life, and you took her name to get a passport." Craig paused. "I went up to Welburton today. I talked to your brother-in-law."

"Oh no!" Paula breathed.

There was a tap on the door and the housekeeper entered the room. "Excuse

369

me, sir," she said, addressing the colonel. "There's a Detective Chief Inspector Franklin asking to see Mrs. Renton."

Standing in the doorway, Craig looked round the bar. The case was nearly over. He had had a long talk to Franklin, and only a few loose ends still remained to be tied up. Paula was at the police divisional headquarters at Lambsdown, officially helping the police with their enquiries, and no doubt the colonel would engage some high powered solicitor from London who would advise her to say nothing. Whether she accepted his advice depended on her mental state as much as anything; she had been near breaking point at one stage this evening.

The bar was only moderately busy, at nine o'clock most of the early drinkers had left and the last minute charge hadn't yet begun. Craig saw Winters standing at the bar chatting to the plump barmaid and walked over to join him.

"Hallo there," Winters said cheerfully. "You made it then?"

"Yes," Craig agreed. He saw that Winters' glass was empty. "What are you drinking?"

"Crown. I'll get them."

Craig didn't want Winters to buy him a drink. "That's all right," he said. He smiled at the girl. "Two pints of Crown, please, love."

She drew the beer and he paid her.

"Everything go all right?" Winters enquired.

"Everything?"

"I thought you said you had to see somebody."

Craig was pretty sure he hadn't said so. He suspected that the other man was trying to pump him to learn where he had been since they met at the garage.

"Yes," he answered. "Fine. Let's go over there."

Leaving Winters to follow him, he made his way over to a table near the door and sat down with his back to the room.

Winters took the chair facing him. "Cheers," he said, raising his glass.

"Cheers." The beer tasted just the same as it had done every time he had drunk Crown over the last week, Craig thought. A constant in a changing world. But it shouldn't do, not this evening. "The police have taken Mrs. Renton to the station at Lambsdown," he said.

Winters stared at him over the rim of his glass. Then, slowly, he put the glass down on the table. If he was shocked or startled, there was no sign of it; Paula might have been a stranger. "Paula?" he said. And now he sounded incredulous. "What for?"

"They think she was involved in the murders of Mary Thornton and Ruth Adamson."

"Paula? You must be joking. I don't believe it." Winters toyed with his glass. "She can't have killed Ruth, she was with me."

"They don't think she was. They have an idea that your staying at the Crosslands at the same time was fixed to provide an alibi." Craig could almost see the other man's brain working behind his expressionless features.

"Why should she need an alibi?" Winters asked.

Their eyes met.

"She didn't," Craig said. "You did."

"Me?" Winters forced a laugh. "What for?"

"When you killed Mrs. Adamson. You killed both of them, Mrs. Renton had nothing to do with it. It was you followed Mary on to the water bus and pushed her into the canal. But it didn't work, they pulled her out. So you had to try again. That evening on the Orient Express when we were talking in the bar before dinner you waited until Mary and most of the rest of the party except Michael Paget had come in, then you said you had to speak to him, and you went out. You walked along the corridor to Mary's cabin and put the drug you'd taken with you from here in her orange juice. That's what you'd planned to do all along, but when you got out there pushing her into the canal seemed simpler and safer. Afterwards you walked back to the dining car as if you'd been talking to Paget. You were the last two in."

"You're mad," Winters said. He spoke lightly, but the muscles of his face were tense and there were beads of sweat on his forehead. "Why should I want to kill Mary? I hardly knew her."

"Because Mrs. Renton told you she was going to bring the Renton family tree up to date, and she was worried she would find out that her real husband was still alive and she had never been legally married to the colonel."

"You think she'd tell me a thing like that?"

"I think so. You're her son."

People were talking all round them, but Craig was unaware of it. It was as though he and Winters were isolated. There was a new tension in the atmosphere, and suddenly it seemed very quiet.

"Hers and Terry Benson's," he went on. "You were born while she was in Holloway. Her sister Gwen and her husband adopted you and gave you their name, Winters. I talked to Brian this afternoon. He said that after his wife died he told you what he could about your parents. He knew his sister-in-law had changed her name and gone to France to work, and that she'd married a man named Renton she met out there, but that was about all. Neither he nor his wife had seen her again after she went to France; she cut herself right off from everything connected with her past. That suited them, they'd never liked her and they looked on you as their own son. Do you remember, you told me on the Orient Express that you used to go home on Fridays on the five twenty-five from St. Pancras? I looked it up, that train goes to Leicester." Craig paused. "I wondered why Mrs. Renton looked so annoyed when you called her 'Paula' just afterwards. She's old fashioned in some ways, and she didn't like her son calling her by her Christian name."

"Go on," Winters said, unconsciously echoing the colonel.

"Your mother played her role to perfection. She really became what she wanted to be, the lady at the big house, liked and admired by everybody who knew her. And wealthy. Until you turned up. I suppose it was sheer luck you getting that job at the brewery, but it didn't make any difference; you could have got in touch with her easily enough if you were still in London. It must have been a shock for her when you did."

"It was a hell of a shock." Winters grinned at the memory. He seemed to have recovered some of his poise.

"You didn't have to blackmail her, whatever you'd intended. She's been giving you money every month because she feels guilty about having nothing to do with you all those years. And you reckoned you could count on a hefty lump sum when the colonel died, with more to follow. Then Mary Thornton came along. You saw yourself losing everything. If your mother's past came out, and the fact that she and the colonel weren't really married, he might throw

376

her out. She could even go to gaol for bigamy. You may not have minded her going to gaol but you couldn't stand the thought of not getting all that money. So you decided to kill Mary before she could do any damage."

"What a load of old cobblers," Winters said. "Why am I supposed to have killed Ruth Adamson?"

"Because you were desperate to get hold of Mary's notebooks; you were afraid there might be something about your mother in them. Mary told you at dinner that evening in Venice that she'd left them behind. You and I and Leila Davidson were the only ones there."

"I thought it seemed a bit too careful, you and Mrs. Renton having separate rooms at the Crosslands if you were having it off with her. Why didn't you just go to another hotel where you weren't known? But you weren't, and there was never any question of you sharing a room. About two-thirty in the morning you slipped out and drove down here to break into Mrs. Adamson's house. I don't suppose you meant to kill her then, but she heard something and came to see what it was. You could have just pushed her out of the way, but she recognised you, and you knew that if she found the notebooks had gone, it would link you with what happened to Mary. So you killed her. You spent the next three or four hours somewhere a safe distance from here, then you drove back to Town, parked near the hotel, and strolled in as though you'd been for a walk before breakfast. Your mother didn't want you to go to Venice, did she?"

"Not much, no," Winters agreed.

"She knew you weren't interested in Agatha Christie, and she was afraid you were going to get up to something. When Mary was pushed into the water she was scared stiff. But after Mary died, and everybody believed she'd committed suicide, she was so relieved it showed. Then the colonel told her that Mary was murdered, and the same person had killed Ruth Adamson, and she was worried sick. She clung to the hope that it wasn't you as long as she could, but once she knew the truth this evening she wasn't prepared to shield a murderer. Not even her son."

"It was her idea she stayed at the Crosslands," Winters said. "Not mine. She talked me into it. She must have killed Ruth."

Craig was too experienced to be shocked by the other man's attempt to shift the blame on to his mother. Maybe, after the way she had neglected him all these years, he felt he owed her nothing.

"It won't work," he told him. "One of the porters at the Crosslands saw you slip out, and a police patrol spotted your car parked in a lay-by with you in it soon after four."

"They can't have done," Winters declared. "I didn't park in a lay-by, I — " He stopped abruptly and for the first time fear showed in his eyes. "They'll never prove it."

"I wouldn't count on it," Craig told him. He wished he felt as confident as he sounded. He looked past Winters at the two men who had come in a few minutes before and now were approaching their table.

Winters saw him and turned.

"Clive Winters?" the taller of the two asked. Winters didn't answer. "I am Detective Chief Inspector Franklin and this is Detective Sergeant Salisbury. As a result of information we have received I must ask you to come with us to the police station to answer some questions concerning the death of Mrs. Ruth Adamson. You will be given the opportunity to make a statement if you wish to do so."

Winters spoke then. "I don't have much choice, do I?" he said.

Neither of the policemen answered, and he stood up. "'Bye, Alan."

Craig watched him walk away, a slight, dapper figure between the two tall detectives. Because of his greed two women were dead and two other lives shattered. Paula might go to prison for bigamy, although Craig thought it unlikely, but it was Colonel Renton he was sorriest for. Whatever happened, the old man would never be able to put the pieces together again.

He drained the beer left in his glass, went out to the phone box in the lobby and dialled Leila's number. But although he hung on for over a minute, there was no answer.

THE END

MURDER TO BURN
Laurie Mantell

Sergeants Steven Arrow and Lance Brendon, of the New Zealand police force, come upon a woman's body in the water. When the dead woman is identified they begin to realise that they are investigating a complex fraud.

YOU CAN HELP ME
Maisie Birmingham

Whilst running the Citizens' Advice Bureau, Kate Weatherley is attacked with no apparent motive. Then the body of one of her clients is found in her room.

DAGGERS DRAWN
Margaret Carr

Stacey Manston was the kind of girl who could take most things in her stride, but three murders were something different . . .

THE MONTMARTRE MURDERS
Richard Grayson

Inspector Gautier of Sûreté investigates the disappearance of artist Théo, the heir to a fortune.

GRIZZLY TRAIL
Gwen Moffat

Miss Pink, alone in the Rockies, helps in a search for missing hikers, solves two cruel murders and has the most terrifying experience of her life when she meets a grizzly bear!

BLINDMAN'S BLUFF
Margaret Carr

Kate Deverill had considered suicide. It was one way out — and preferable to being murdered.

BEGOTTEN MURDER
Martin Carroll

When Susan Phillips joined her aunt on a voyage of 12,000 miles from her home in Melbourne, she little knew their arrival would germinate the seeds of murder planted long ago.

WHO'S THE TARGET?
Margaret Carr

Three people whom Abby could identify as her parents' murderers wanted her dead, but she decided that maybe Jason could have been the target.

THE LOOSE SCREW
Gerald Hammond

After a motor smash, Beau Pepys and his cousin Jacqueline, her fiancé and dotty mother, suspect that someone had prearranged the death of their friend. But who, and why?

CASE WITH THREE HUSBANDS
Margaret Erskine

Was it a ghost of one of Rose Bonner's late husbands that gave her old Aunt Agatha such a terrible shock and then murdered her in her bed?

THE END OF THE RUNNING
Alan Evans

Lang continued to push the men and children on and on. Behind them were the men who were hunting them down, waiting for the first signs of exhaustion before they pounced.

CARNABY AND THE HIJACKERS
Peter N. Walker

When Commander Pigeon assigns Detective Sergeant Carnaby-King to prevent a raid on a bullion-carrying passenger train, he knows that there are traitors in high positions.

TREAD WARILY AT MIDNIGHT
Margaret Carr

If Joanna Morse hadn't been so hasty she wouldn't have been involved in the accident.

TOO BEAUTIFUL TO DIE
Martin Carroll

There was a grave in the churchyard to prove Elizabeth Weston was dead. Alive, she presented a problem. Dead, she could be forgotten. Then, in the eighth year of her death she came back. She was beautiful, but she had to die.

IN COLD PURSUIT
Ursula Curtiss

In Mexico, Mary and her cousin Jenny each encounter strange men, but neither of them realises that one of these men is obsessed with revenge and murder. But which one?

LITTLE DROPS OF BLOOD
Bill Knox

It might have been just another unfortunate road accident but a few little drops of blood pointed to murder.

GOSSIP TO THE GRAVE
Jonathan Burke

Jenny Clark invented Simon Sherborne because her daily gossip column was getting dull. Then Simon appeared at a party — in the flesh! And Jenny finds herself involved in murder.

HARRIET FAREWELL
Margaret Erskine

Wealthy Theodore Buckler had planned a magnificent Guy Fawkes Day celebration. He hadn't planned on murder.

SANCTUARY ISLE
Bill Knox

Chief Detective Inspector Colin Thane and Detective Inspector Phil Moss are sent to a bird sanctuary off the coast of Argyll to investigate the murder of the warden.

THE SNOW ON THE BEN
Ian Stuart

Although on holiday in the Highlands, Chief Inspector Hamish MacLeod begins an investigation when a pistol shot shatters the quiet of his solitary morning walk.

HARD CONTRACT
Basil Copper

Private detective Mike Farraday is hired to obtain settlement of a debt from Minsky. But Minsky is killed before Mike can get to him. A spate of murders follows.

VICIOUS CIRCLE
Alan Evans

Crawford finds himself on the run and hunted in a strange land, wanting only to find his son but prepared to pay any cost.

DEATH ON A QUIET BEACH
Simon Challis

For Thurston, the blonde on the beach was routine. Within hours he had another body to deal with, and suddenly it wasn't routine any more.

DEATH IN THE SCILLIES
Howard Charles Davis

What had happened to the yachtsman whose boat had drifted on to the Seven Sisters Reef? Who is recruiting a bodyguard for a millionaire and why should bodyguards be needed in the Scillies.

THE SCORPION TRAP
Alfred Handley

Why was the postman shot on a country road? Things began to happen — such as blackmail, the gift of a Scorpion and a tangled web leading back into the past.

DRINK! FOR ONCE DEAD
Alan Sewart

How could a dead man's fingerprints turn up on a fresh beer glass? Chamberlane discovered some very disturbing possibilities about the science of fingerprint identification.

DARE THE DEVIL
Margaret Carr

Dan didn't expect to find himself involved in witchcraft and devil worship, but he had to help Leonora for she was to be sacrificed by order of her dead husband!

CINDERELLA SPY
Philip Daniels

Sally Driscoll was asked by Whitehall to impersonate drug courier Martha for one day. She was plunged into a nightmare world where life was cheap, and she would need all her courage if she was to survive.

MANTRAP
Alan Evans

Cragg and Frayne had not intended to stay, but Collins could not be persuaded to fly them out. They make the attempt but their jeep is destroyed by bandits.

THE HOUSE ON THE FEN
Claire Rayner

Harriet found herself running away from the cruel husband she feared. She was free for the first time in her life, on a train bound for London.